"Take Me Off The Market," Dylan Taunted With A Sexy Grin.

Alisa took a quick shallow breath at the audacity of his seductive offer. "I might be able to take you off the market, but I don't think I have what it takes to *keep* you off the market."

His humor faded. "Is that what you would expect from what you've come to know of me since your accident?"

That stopped her. Her mind went blank.

"If it is, you haven't been paying attention," he said with a finality that alternately terrified and relieved her. She wondered if the next words out of his mouth would be goodbye.

"But that's okay," Dylan finally said, his jaw clenching with impatience. "I'm leaving right now, but I'll be back. A long time ago, I was once called that bad penny. A bad penny just keeps showing up. Well, Alisa, I'm your bad penny."

Dear Reader,

Welcome to the world of Silhouette Desire, where you can indulge yourself every month with romances that can only be described as passionate, powerful and provocative!

Fabulous BJ James brings you June's MAN OF THE MONTH with *A Lady for Lincoln Cade*. In promising to take care of an ex-flame—and the widow of his estranged friend— Lincoln Cade discovers she has a child. Bestselling author Leanne Banks offers another title in her MILLION DOLLAR MEN miniseries with *The Millionaire's Secret Wish*. When a former childhood sweetheart gets amnesia, a wealthy executive sees his chance to woo her back.

Desire is thrilled to present another exciting miniseries about the scandalous Fortune family with FORTUNES OF TEXAS: THE LOST HEIRS. Anne Marie Winston launches the series with *A Most Desirable M.D.*, in which a doctor and nurse share a night of passion that leads to marriage! Dixie Browning offers a compelling story about a sophisticated businessman who falls in love with a plain, plump woman while stranded on a small island in *More to Love*. Cathleen Galitz's *Wyoming Cinderella* features a young woman whose life is transformed when she becomes nanny to the children of her brooding, rich neighbor. And Kathie DeNosky offers her hero a surprise when he discovers a one-night stand leads to pregnancy and true love in *His Baby Surprise*.

Indulge yourself with all six Desire titles—and see details inside about our exciting new contest, "Silhouette Makes You a Star."

Enjoy!

Joan Marlow Golan

Joan Marlow Golan
Senior Editor, Silhouette Desire

Please address questions and book requests to:
Silhouette Reader Service
U.S.: 3010 Walden Ave., P.O. Box 1325, Buffalo, NY 14269
Canadian: P.O. Box 609, Fort Erie, Ont. L2A 5X3

The Millionaire's Secret Wish

LEANNE BANKS

Silhouette® Desire®

Published by Silhouette Books

America's Publisher of Contemporary Romance

This book is dedicated to my daughter, Alisa.
You are such a precious gift.

 **SILHOUETTE BOOKS**

ISBN 0-373-76370-0

THE MILLIONAIRE'S SECRET WISH

Books by Leanne Banks

Silhouette Desire

Ridge: The Avenger #987
*The Five-Minute Bride #1058
*The Troublemaker Bride #1070
*The You-Can't-Make-Me Bride #1082
†Millionaire Dad #1166
†The Lone Rider Takes a Bride #1172
†Thirty-Day Fiancé #1179
The Secretary and the Millionaire #1208
‡‡Her Forever Man #1267
‡‡The Doctor Wore Spurs #1280
‡‡Expecting His Child #1292
Bride of Fortune #1311
ΔExpecting the Boss's Baby #1338
ΔMillionaire Husband #1352
ΔThe Millionaire's Secret Wish #1370

Silhouette Special Edition

A Date with Dr. Frankenstein #983
Expectant Father #1028

* How To Catch a Princess
† The Rulebreakers
‡‡ Lone Star Families: The Logans
Δ Million-Dollar Men

LEANNE BANKS

is a national number-one bestselling author of romance. She lives in her native Virginia with her husband, son and daughter. Recognized for both her sensual and humorous writing with two Career Achievement Awards from *Romantic Times Magazine,* Leanne likes creating a story with a few grins, a generous kick of sensuality and characters that hang around after the book is finished. Leanne believes romance readers are the best readers in the world because they understand that love is the greatest miracle of all. You can write to her at P.O. Box 1442, Midlothian, VA 23113. A SASE for a reply would be greatly appreciated.

SILHOUETTE MAKES YOU A STAR!

Feel like a star with Silhouette.
Look for the exciting details of our new contest
inside all of these fabulous Silhouette novels:

Romance

#1522 An Officer and a Princess
Carla Cassidy

#1523 Her Tycoon Boss
Karen Rose Smith

THE TEXAS BROTHERHOOD
#1524 A Child for Cade
Patricia Thayer

AN OLDER MAN
#1525 The Baby Season
Alice Sharpe

#1526 Blind-Date Bride
Myrna Mackenzie

#1527 The Littlest Wrangler
Belinda Barnes

Special Edition

#1399 The Stranger in Room 205
Gina Wilkins

#1400 Shelter in a Soldier's Arms
Susan Mallery

#1401 The M.D. Meets His Match
Marie Ferrarella

#1402 Invitation to a Wedding
Peggy Webb

#1403 Her Sister's Secret Son
Lisette Belisle

#1404 Almost a Bride
Patricia McLinn

Desire

#1369 A Lady for Lincoln Cade
BJ James

#1370 The Millionaire's Secret Wish
Leanne Banks

#1371 A Most Desirable M.D.
Anne Marie Winston

#1372 More to Love
Dixie Browning

#1373 Wyoming Cinderella
Cathleen Galitz

#1374 His Baby Surprise
Kathie DeNosky

Intimate Moments

#1081 Hard-Headed Texan
Candace Camp

#1082 Familiar Stranger
Sharon Sala

#1083 Daddy with a Badge
Paula Detmer Riggs

#1084 Moonglow, Texas
Mary McBride

#1085 Cops and...Lovers?
Linda Castillo

#1086 Dangerous Attraction
Susan Vaughan

Prologue

"**P**ayday is gonna come for this, and you may not like the way you get paid."

"I know," Dylan Barrow said to one of his best friends in the world, Michael Hawkins. "But I have to do it."

"When she regains her memory and remembers who you are and that you didn't tell her the truth, you're gonna be toast," Michael warned him as he signaled the bartender at O'Malley's in St. Albans, Virginia, for another round of drinks.

"He's not technically lying to her, though," Justin Langdon, Dylan's other longtime friend said.

"He's omitting," Michael said ominously. "Justin, you haven't been married long enough to know how much trouble you can get into for the sin of omission.''

Dylan felt his gut twist and took a long swallow of beer. ''Alisa needs me. Her mother's on an extended trip to Europe. She doesn't have anyone else right now.''

Michael sighed and shook his head. ''Hard to believe Alisa Jennings is the same girl who used to sneak cookies to us when we lived at the Granger's Home for Boys and that her mother worked in the cafeteria. What does she remember?''

''Bits and pieces,'' Dylan said. ''Sometimes I look at her and I can see she feels totally lost, but lately she's acting more frustrated and angry. The doctors say the frustration is normal, and they'd rather see that than depression.''

''In her own way she was always a fighter,'' Justin mused.

''A fighter? Maybe like a butterfly. She was always so sensitive, never wanted to hurt anyone's feelings.''

''But she always fought to keep up with you,'' Justin said. ''Remember how long she practiced so she wouldn't be afraid of catching the ball. The poor kid got a black eye one time.''

Dylan remembered the same incident. A dozen more flitted through his mind. When he'd lived at Granger's, Alisa had always been like a cool drink of water for him. Gentle, soothing and constant. Her constant presence had been his downfall. Without realizing it, he'd relied on her and taken for granted that she would always be there. Their childhood friendship blossomed and they'd become teenage sweethearts just before her widowed mother remarried, precipitating a move out of state.

When she'd left, Dylan had been shocked at the empty feeling that never seemed to leave him, and he'd vowed never to rely on another person that way.

"You never gave the full story on what happened when you two got together in college," Justin said with an insight that made Dylan uncomfortable.

"It ended badly," Dylan said, remembering Alisa's tears and the sense of betrayal he'd seen in her eyes. She had shut him out of her life and never looked back. The maturity gained by passing time had given him painful clarity of the fact that a woman like Alisa only came along once in a man's life, if he was damn lucky.

"I kinda got that impression since she hardly speaks to you when we all get together," Justin said dryly, then glanced at his watch. "But don't worry. I won't grill you tonight. One of the twins has chicken pox and I think our house could be turned upside down for the next month. I don't want Amy to start her Joan of Arc routines, so I need to keep this short."

Despite the heaviness of the conversation, Dylan couldn't help shaking his head in wonder. Justin, who had been antimarriage and antichildren, had become a proponent of marriage and a devoted father to his three adopted children. "You amaze me," Dylan said. "To think it all started with your ulcer."

Justin gave a lopsided grin. "Yeah. Amy saved my life in more ways than one. She wants to know who donated the money to her afterschool program for underprivileged kids. So far, I've dodged her, but her creative persistence could be the death of me," he said and took a swig of beer.

Michael chuckled and dipped his head as if he understood. "I have the same problem with Kate. It's hell keeping my involvement in the Millionaires' Club secret from my wife."

Dylan shrugged. "We set it up to be a secret charity, but if you guys want to tell your wives, I don't have a problem with it."

Justin and Michael were silent for a full moment. "That would mean Amy might not be nearly so creative in trying to get me to spill the beans," Justin said. He exchanged a knowing glance with Michael.

Michael chuckled. "We'll just keep things the way they are. It's your turn for our next project," he said to Dylan. "How's it coming?"

"Slow but sure," he said. "I want to find a way to start a bioengineering research project with Remington Pharmaceuticals."

"I knew this was going to be expensive," Justin said, taking a deep swallow of beer. "I don't know if our pockets are gonna be deep enough for this."

Dylan lifted his hand. "Hold on," he said, knowing that despite the fact that Justin was a millionaire, his friend would always be a tightwad at heart. "You guys know my story. The father I didn't know existed until he died left me a position on the board at Remington Pharmaceuticals as part of my inheritance. The other board members resented the hell out of that, so I haven't done much except stay out of the way and offer a suggestion once in a blue moon. I placed my votes as favors. Now it's payback time.''

Michael looked at Dylan in surprised admiration. ''You dog,'' he said with a grin. ''You let them get comfortable with you, made them owe you, and now you're going to lower the boom with this bioengineering research project. Good strategy.''

Dylan took that as high praise since Michael had built an Internet start-up company which had turned him into a multimillionaire. He knew some people confused his easygoing nature with apathy of his position, wealth and ambition. But Dylan had his own goals in life and he'd learned the hard way to stick with what was truly important. ''I decided from the start to save my energy for the battles that really mattered to me.''

Michael nodded. ''Is this similar to you taking Alisa to your home to recover?''

''Yeah,'' he said, thinking the stakes were higher with Alisa than they were with the bioengineering project. In his gut Dylan knew this was his last shot with her.

''I wouldn't want to be in your shoes. What do you think is gonna come of all of this? That you'll earn her undying gratitude by taking care of her while she's recovering from amnesia?''

"Undying gratitude would be a step up from her undying disdain," Dylan muttered, thinking of how Alisa hadn't given him the time of day for the past several years. But he wanted more, more than he wanted to admit to himself, let alone his friends. He took a long drink and felt the rightness of his dead-on commitment resonate inside him. "I've never been more sure of something I had to do than this. She may hate me later, but she needs me now."

One

Was she talkative or quiet?

Was she a flirt or a tease with men?

Or was she demure?

She stared into the mirror in her hospital bathroom and familiarized herself with her features again, hoping for a lightbulb of recognition. Green eyes, straight-as-a-stick blond hair, clear skin with the exception of the fading multicolored bruises on her forehead. She had a couple of cowlicks throughout her hair from the places where the surgeon had stitched her wounds.

She'd been told her name was Alisa Jennings. She knew she spoke French well enough to be employed as a corporate interpreter. On a particularly dismal, empty day, a visitor had supplied her with artists' drawing materials and she'd learned she had a little talent.

She knew she was twenty-six years old and stood five feet six inches. What she didn't know about herself could fill a book. What she didn't know about herself made her want to scream. In fact, she'd done a little screaming during a recent session with the hospital psychiatrist. The psychiatrist had remained so calm Alisa had wanted to throw a lunch tray against the wall.

Alisa might not know much at the moment, but she knew there was power in knowing one's self, one's history, one's weaknesses and strengths. She didn't have that power, and she hated the absence of it.

She hated the constant question marks. Who was she, anyway? Was she a wicked, selfish woman? She supposed she couldn't be totally wicked considering how she'd gotten into this mess in the first place. She'd been chasing a little boy's dog.

So, was she a sap? That might be worse than wicked, she thought.

She wanted the answers to all her questions and she wanted them now, but her brain refused, no matter how hard she searched.

She rolled her eyes and stuck her tongue out at herself. "What a pain."

"Did you hurt something?" a male voice asked from behind her.

Alisa immediately recognized the voice. She may

not remember diddly about the years of friendship Dylan had told her they'd shared, but she knew his voice because he'd visited her at the hospital every day since she'd been here.

She scooted out of the bathroom. ''I was thinking about bonking my head against the wall to see if I could shake anything loose from my stingy memory.''

He winced at the image. ''I think you've done enough head bonking for a while.'' He lifted his hand and barely brushed his fingers over the bruise on her forehead.

She stood still, watching him while he touched her. He stood at least five inches taller than her, with broad shoulders and a well-toned body. His brown hair was shot with sparks of gold from the sun, showing he spent time outdoors. He moved with an athletic grace and emanated an easy, careless kind of masculine charm that she'd noticed drew the attention of many of the female hospital staff. His intense, intelligent hazel eyes belied the reckless smile.

In short, her long-time friend was one hot man, and Alisa wondered how she'd managed all these years to keep from having a crush on him. Perhaps she would ask him sometime. She could blame the question on her amnesia, she thought wryly. The bane of her present existence should be good for something.

''Ready to go?'' he asked.

Alisa sighed. Dylan had offered his home to her while she continued to recover. Although she wished she was strong enough to return to her apartment, she knew she needed a little more time to get up to speed. Several people had visited her during her stay in the hospital, but Dylan was the one person who seemed least uncomfortable with her loss of memory. "Yes. Was I always impatient?"

He gave her an assessing glance. "Impatient?"

"Impatient with unanswered questions about myself. Impatient with getting tired every day and needing a nap in the afternoon," she said, picking up her small tote bag.

Dylan reached for the tote. She resisted.

His lips twitched. "Are you sure you're not asking if you've always been independent edging toward contrary?" he asked, extending his hand toward the open door.

"Are we splitting hairs?" she asked, walking with him to the elevator. She waved to the nurses at the station. They'd said their goodbyes earlier. She would never forget their kindness.

"I wouldn't choose the word *impatient*," he said, punching the elevator button. "I think you like being in control of your world and you're not right now."

She glanced at him as they stepped inside and the doors slid closed. "If you wouldn't choose *impatient*, what would you choose?"

"*Independent*," he repeated. "At times *fearless*."

"I'm betting the latter has gotten me into trouble a few times," she said.

"A few times," he said.

She wondered if that trouble had ever been romantic. "How was I with men?" she asked.

Dylan gave her a double take. "With men?"

"Yes. Was I fearless with men? I know I wasn't married. Was I ever engaged? Did I ever get my heart broken? Was I the piney type to sit home by myself on a Saturday night or did I love them and leave them?"

Dylan's gut tightened at her questions. "You were engaged once, but you broke it off. I think you may have gotten your heart broken once," he said, certain he'd been the responsible party. "I've never known you to be piney, but I can't comment much on your love life over the past few years because you didn't discuss it much."

"Closemouthed, huh?" she said. "Darn. Well, what happened when I got my heart broken?"

"You were younger. He was immature and didn't appreciate what he had with you."

"You're saying he didn't deserve me," she said.

"He didn't," Dylan said, knowing again he was speaking of himself. "You dumped him, and when he came around again, you wouldn't give him the time of day."

"Good for me," she said with firm approval.

Dylan felt a twist of dark humor. Alisa might feel as if she'd lost her footing, but in many ways she was still the same. Without knowing it, she'd just informed him that when she remembered who he was, she would leave him again. He figured he had an icicle's chance in hell of changing her mind, but changing her mind wasn't his purpose, he reminded himself. His purpose was to provide an environment for her to heal.

They stepped out of the elevator, and she turned quickly to look at him. Her green gaze searched his. In her eyes he saw kindness and humor rather than the cool indifference he'd endured for years. "You may grow weary of giving history lessons about Alisa to Alisa," she warned him in a husky voice that seduced him from the inside out. "Promise you'll let me know when you get tired of me."

Dylan swallowed a chuckle. If only he could have grown tired of this woman, his romantic life would have been a helluva lot more satisfying. "I promise," he said, and led her to his car.

"You have a beautiful home," Alisa said as she sipped lemonade on a porch that overlooked the swimming pool. It was a hot day, and the water tempted her.

"There's a swimsuit in the things I arranged to have picked up from the store," he said.

She grinned. "I must be obvious. Did you catch me drooling?"

"No, but I thought you might be more comfortable diving in with a swimsuit instead of the clothes you're wearing."

She stood, struggling with another scratchy unanswered question. "I know I swim, but I'm not sure how well."

He shrugged. "You're a good swimmer, but just don't jump into the deep end first."

A millimeter of her tension eased away. "This is going to sound strange, but you make having amnesia easier."

He gave her a doubtful look. "How?"

"It's not a big deal that I remember very little about myself," she said.

"The important things are settled. You're alive and you're going to be okay. Your marbles just got shook up a little bit," he said with the reckless flash of teeth that made women's hearts turn over.

But not *her* heart, Alisa told herself despite the odd little fluttering sensation in her chest. "And what if all the marbles don't go back to the way they were?"

"The important ones will," he said with such an easy assurance that it somehow gave her confidence.

He had no idea what a gift his belief in her was. Alisa was having a tough time knowing what to believe. Her task to put her marbles back in place was so huge she sometimes couldn't see beyond it, but when she did, she always saw Dylan, and she was starting to want to know him as much as she wanted to know herself.

After several laps, a bone-deep weariness hit her like a ton of bricks, and she dragged herself from the pool to take several deep breaths. A shadow crossed over her and she glanced up at Dylan.

"Did you consider swimming just one or two laps to start instead of training for a two-hundred-meter sprint?"

She glanced down at his bare feet just inches from her hand. "Not once. Please leave and let me collapse in peace."

"Not on my property," he said. "You want me to give you a lift to that lounge chair in the shade?"

She shook her head, eyeing the lounge, embarrassed by her lack of stamina. "No. I'll go in a min—" She broke off when he tucked one of his arms beneath her legs and the other behind her back. "You really don't need to—" She didn't finish before he carried her the short distance across the concrete and set her down on the lounge.

Frustrated, she covered her eyes and felt them burn with the threat of tears. She heard Dylan give a muffled oath.

"You want me to put you back on the side of the pool?" he asked.

She shook her head, but kept her eyes covered. A wayward tear streamed down her cheek.

"Alisa, send a smoke signal or a pigeon. How can I help?"

She took a shallow breath and tried to rid herself of the heavy feeling in her chest. "Don't you know children cry when they get overtired?"

"I hadn't thought of it until you mentioned it," he said.

"I just want to be able to get through the day without needing a nap," she said, swiping her cheek and looking up at him.

"That will happen in time," he said. "But since you've been laying in a hospital bed on your nice, young rear end for four weeks, you're going to need a few days before you can enter the Olympics." He lifted his hand when she opened her mouth to interrupt. "The reason I brought you here was so you could recover. Your body has been through a lot. Take it slow and don't torture yourself."

"But I want to be stronger," she said, frustration flashing through her again.

"Being hardheaded isn't going to make you strong," he told her.

"Are you lecturing me?"

"Yeah, and it's my prerogative since I'm your—" he narrowed his eyes "—friend. Take it slow."

"And if I don't want to go slow?"

"Then you can keep feeling just like you do right now or you can end up back in the hospital." He muttered another oath. "The shrink warned me you might be difficult to handle, but I didn't expect this."

Alisa gaped at him. "Difficult? How?"

"Argumentative, emotional, frustrated, full of questions."

Temper gave her the energy to stand. "I'm not difficult," she told him. "I may not know much about myself, but I know I'm not difficult or argumentative or emotional.'' She met his gaze and her defense sat between them like a flat tire. She *had* been difficult, argumentative and emotional, she realized when her mind cleared and the moment stretched between them.

"I'm not difficult,'' she said in an even tone that required all her self-control, ''except when I've been in a hospital for a month and I'm recovering from amnesia. That's the only time,'' she told him in no uncertain terms, ''I'm difficult. And even then I'm not very difficult at all.''

She watched him bite his lip and hoped against hope he wouldn't grin or chuckle because her hand was itching and she would give new meaning to the word *difficult*. ''The reason I came down was to tell you the cook is preparing blackened fish for dinner. She wanted to know if you like spicy food.''

Alisa closed her eyes for a moment and concentrated on spicy food. Instinctively she knew she liked spicy food. The doctor had said she would likely recall most of her preferences, but might have a more difficult time remembering what she'd eaten for breakfast or where she had left her keys. A short-term memory deficit was one more thing that shredded her already slim patience supply. She was combating some of her memory problems by working crossword puzzles and making lists. She looked at Dylan, knowing she would need to be as sharp as a laser to keep up with him. She was determined to make that happen.

"Yes," she finally said, meeting his expectant gaze. "Don't ask me how I know. I just do," she said and walked toward her room. Maybe a nap would help after all.

"You're quiet," Dylan said as they sat on the terrace after dinner. "Are you tired…or pouting?"

"Neither. I don't think I'm much of a pouter. I'm just thinking. I remembered something about work just before dinner."

Sipping an after-dinner whisky, he glanced at her. "What did you remember?"

"One of the Frenchmen whose work I interpret hits on me every time he visits the States."

"How do you handle it?"

"I joke with him and tell him he would break my heart. I think he enjoys the chase. I think most men may be a little like that," she mused.

"A little like what?"

"Enjoy the chase more than they enjoy a real relationship with a woman." She glanced at him. "Do you?"

Dylan took a swallow of whisky and rolled his shoulder as if he were uncomfortable with the question. "I haven't done much chasing."

Her curiosity piqued by his incomplete answer, she studied him for a long moment until the light dawned. "You are the chasee instead of the chaser. That shouldn't surprise me. You're good-looking, wealthy and not a total jerk.''

He gave her a sideways glance. "High praise," he muttered. "Being the chasee has its downside.''

She laughed. "Poor Dylan. Surrounded by women. It must be terrible.''

"Do I look like I'm surrounded by women?" he asked. "It looks to me as if I'm being tormented by just one.''

She laughed again. "Have you always been chased? What do you think it is? Were you always good-looking and charming?''

He lifted his lips in a sexy smile that made her heart flutter. "Good-looking and charming. High praise again. Have I always been chased by women? Let's just say it's always been easy to find a date. Why? Beats the hell out of me. But I've learned an important lesson. Quality is more important than quantity. I'd rather be chased by the one right woman than several not-right women. And when I am chased by the right woman, she will catch me.''

"But what if you need to be the chaser to get the right woman?''

His eyes grew serious. "I can do that," he said with quiet masculine assurance that did strange things to her nerve endings.

More questions about him filled her mind, but for some reason she wasn't sure she wanted all the answers yet. Alisa knew she wouldn't be able to learn everything she wanted to know about this man in one evening or one month. She reached for his glass of whisky. "Mind if I try it?"

Surprise crossed his face. "Go ahead."

She took a sip and felt the liquid burn down her throat.

"Like it?"

Making a face, she shook her head and pushed the glass back toward him. "How can you drink that?"

"It's an acquired taste. Twenty-five-year-old whisky."

"Geez, then fire a cannon and bury it," she said, and felt a ripple of pleasure that she made him laugh.

He could turn a woman's head, she thought. For a moment she feared he would turn hers, then quickly dismissed the possibility. He'd said they were friends, but Alisa wondered how a woman could be friends with Dylan without wanting more. There must be a reason. She would learn that reason soon.

Her shriek woke him from a sound sleep. Dylan sat straight up in bed. Another shriek broke the silence of the night, and he immediately rose from his bed and walked down the hallway to the room where Alisa was staying. The doctor had warned him about her nightmares.

Not bothering to knock, he entered the room and, with the aid of moonlight from the window, saw her sitting up with her head in her hands. Her shaky breaths made his gut twist and turn.

"Alisa," he said in a low voice so he wouldn't frighten her. He sat down on the bed beside her.

"Sorry," she said, shuddering. "Bad dream. I don't remember much about the accident when I'm awake, but I've had a few nightmares. I keep seeing a little boy's puppy running into the street. The little boy is on crutches and for some reason I know that dog means everything to him. I run after the dog and an SUV whips around the corner. I try, but I can't run fast enough...."

"The little boy was Timmy," Dylan said, pulling her into his arms. He knew Alisa was strong, but she felt incredibly fragile to him right now. "Timmy is a neighbor kid with cerebral palsy, and you've taken care of him several times to give his single mom a break. You ran after the dog so he wouldn't."

"He sent me pictures he'd painted while I was in the hospital." She took a deep breath and gave a little smile. "The puppy made it just fine, didn't he?"

"Yeah," Dylan muttered. He slid his fingers through her hair and felt the edge of one of her scars. His chest tightened with the memory of that terrible time just after Alisa's accident. He could have lost her for good. The world could have lost her, and that would have been one helluva loss. Even though he'd blown his chances with her, just knowing Alisa existed made him believe in the future.

"Every time I have that dream it scares me. I hate being afraid," she said.

No surprise, he thought, recalling what she'd been

like as a child. Alisa had always fought her fear. "How about a bedtime story?"

She looked up at him, seeming reluctant to pull back from him. Dylan drank in the moment. It had been eons since she'd allowed him to hold her, since she'd wanted him to hold her.

"No puppies or SUVs?"

He shook his head. "No puppies or SUVs. Once upon a time a little girl was surrounded by orphan boys. Day after day, she watched them play baseball. She wanted to play, too, but the boys wouldn't let her."

"Why not?"

"She couldn't catch worth a damn."

"Oh," she said with a grimace. "That's a problem."

"Yep, and she could see it was a problem. She talked one of the boys into teaching her to catch the ball."

"How did she do that?"

Dylan remembered how Alisa had begged and pleaded and finally offered a trade. "That's another bedtime story."

She smiled and relaxed in his arms. "Okay. So what happened?"

"The little girl was afraid of the ball, and the boy told her that until she stopped being afraid of the ball, the other boys wouldn't let her play. The little boy and girl practiced every day, and she started to improve. She got so much better the boys allowed her to play in one of their games.''

''Good,'' she said.

''That's not the end.''

''Oh, then finish the story.''

''In that very first game, a fastball came flying at the little girl. She didn't duck and she didn't bring her glove up fast enough.''

Alisa winced the same way Dylan knew he had winced that day many years ago. ''Oh, no.''

''The ball hit her in the eye, but she somehow still managed to catch the ball. The boys cheered for her. She tried not to cry, but it was very hard. Her eye swelled up right away, and the little boy who taught her to catch felt like crap. He thought she would never play again, and he kinda hoped she wouldn't so she wouldn't get hurt again.''

Dylan remembered how miserable he'd felt when he'd seen Alisa get hurt. Looking at her eye had made his chest feel heavy with guilt.

''If he hadn't taught her to catch, then she wouldn't have gotten hurt,'' he said, remembering the regret like it was yesterday.

''But she wouldn't have known the thrill of winning and the lesson of going all-out for something she wanted.'' She met his gaze, and he saw a glimmer of fearless Alisa in her green eyes. ''Winning is addictive. She played again, didn't she?''

''Yeah, she did. She hated being afraid. You never liked being afraid, Alisa. You always fought it.''

Hope softened the remnants of her nightmare from her face. "So maybe some things stay the same."

"Yeah," he said, knowing her attitude toward him would be one of those things. She closed her eyes, and he sensed the moment she drifted off to sleep. He watched her while she slept, her hair spilling across his arm and her lips gently parted. His heart swelled in his chest. He'd never known how precious her trust was to him until he'd lost it. For this moment she trusted him. But Alisa was recalling new memories every day. It was his job to encourage recollection and healing. It was an ironic twist of fate that he must encourage her toward the very thing that would ultimately turn her against him.

Two

"**I** want to visit my apartment today," Alisa told Dylan as soon as she joined him on the terrace for breakfast.

His gaze played over her from head to toe, acutely reminding her of her femininity. She wondered if he had that effect on every woman and suspected he did. His eyes somehow managed to assess and seduce at the same time. His open-collared shirt revealed a glimpse of his muscular, tanned chest and the sleeves were pushed back to reveal strong forearms. Those same arms had held her last night when she had been afraid, she thought, and felt a ripple of vulnerability. She swallowed over the odd feeling crowding her throat. How did he evoke so many emotions in her?

''No problem,'' he said. ''I can take you to your apartment. You want to eat first?''

Turning her attention from him to the beautifully set table, she smiled. ''Yes, I'd like to eat first. My impatience is showing, isn't it?''

He shrugged. ''Better your impatience than your party panties.''

She blinked at him. An image raced through her mind. ''Party panties are panties with ruffles on the back. I had a pink pair.''

''You did. You also had a white pair with red ruffles.''

She shot him a glance of disapproval. ''How would you know?''

''Because I saw them,'' he said with just a tinge of arrogance.

Curious, she sat beside him at the table and took a croissant from the bread basket. ''Were they on a clothesline or on me?''

''You were definitely wearing them.''

The idea that Dylan had seen her in party panties gave her the strangest urge to squirm. ''I feel certain I didn't show my party pants on purpose. I'm sure there were extenuating circumstances.''

''You could say that,'' he said with a mocking glint in his eyes.

She poured orange juice from a carafe into each of their glasses. ''Okay, I'll bite. What were the extenuating circumstances?''

''You always had to keep up with whatever the

boys were doing,'' he said, pouring milk into a bowl of granola cereal and grabbing a muffin.

''And what were the boys doing this time?''

''It was winter and it had snowed. There was a shortage of sleds, so we made use of trays from the cafeteria. Your mom was so upset I thought she'd give me gruel for a month.'' He shook his head. ''You wanted to use a tray, too, but you had just returned from church so you were wearing your Sunday dress and knee socks. We told you that you couldn't tray sled because you were a girl and you were wearing a dress.''

''I have a feeling I know where this is going,'' she said. ''I decided to prove you wrong, so I got on a tray and raced down the hill.''

Dylan nodded. ''The problem was that your guiding system was a little off. The tray spun around, you slammed into a snowbank face first with your ruffles there for all to see.''

She chewed another bite of croissant and swallowed. ''I don't remember this, but I still feel humiliated. I'll bet you teased me relentlessly about that incident.''

Dylan nodded again as he finished a bowl of granola.

''Are you sure I didn't secretly hate you?''

He shook his head and met her gaze dead-on. ''You adored me,'' he said with a combination of conviction and seduction that gave her a knee-weakening thrill.

Alisa was very glad she was sitting down. "I can't imagine why," she lied and bit into her croissant.

He lifted a dark eyebrow in disbelief. "Why not?"

"If you were one-tenth as cocky as you are now, you had to be insufferable."

"You followed me around like a puppy."

"I absolutely don't remember that," she said.

"You got into trouble with your mother for playing in the rain with me."

She opened her mouth, but a hazy image swam through her mind. She closed her eyes and saw a boy and girl stomping through mud puddles. "You wore tennis shoes," she said. "I ruined my black patent-leather shoes. Your hair was too long. You seemed tall to me," she said, concentrating to milk every detail from the memory.

"It usually was. They gave us haircuts once every three months, but mine grew like a weed."

"You loaned me your camouflage green rain slicker."

"But that didn't do a damn thing for your shoes."

She kept her eyes closed for a long moment and fell back in time. She could hear her mother scolding her, but as a little girl, she was smiling inside. Another adventure with Dylan. Alisa opened her eyes. "Were you always leading me down the road to perdition?"

He rocked his hips slightly in his chair and leaned backward, inadvertently drawing her attention to his thighs. ''I was just teaching you how to have a little fun.''

Swift, hot awareness sped through her. A searing thought that he could teach her about grown-up fun dipped into her mind. She snuffed it out as quickly as it appeared. He was a distracting man, and she didn't need to be distracted from her quest. She needed to concentrate on getting her memory back instead of what kind of lover Dylan would be. Temptation shimmered stubbornly inside her. Alisa took a long swallow of cool orange juice and told herself to focus on healing. Focus on anything but sex with Dylan.

''Breakfast was lovely. Why don't I ever see your cook? I'm beginning to think she's invisible.''

''She likes to set the table, then leave.''

''I'd like to thank her sometime when she comes out of hiding.''

''I'll introduce you.''

''Good.'' She took a deep breath. ''I'm ready to go to my apartment anytime.''

His mouth straightened, and she watched his eyes darken with some emotion she couldn't name. ''Then we'll go,'' he said, and she wondered why his words held a hint of ominous foreboding.

''No pictures on the wall,'' Alisa said in disapproval as she walked through her apartment. She'd hoped for obvious marks of her personality. ''I was hoping for more.''

"You were hoping for billboards with your life history," he said dryly.

She slid a quick glance at him. How did the man read her mind? "It would have been nice."

"You hadn't lived here that long," he reminded her.

She saw a datebook left open on the kitchen counter and dived for it as if it were the Holy Grail. "This may be the closest thing I'll get to a diary." She flipped through the pages. "Busy girl. Cook-out with the Hawkinses on Tuesday night, running date with Paul." She stopped. "Who's Paul?"

He shrugged his shoulders and peered over her shoulder. "No idea. Volunteer work at Granger's," he said, pointing to a notation.

"Business trip to France," she said, and a sound of despair squeaked out of her throat. "A week after my accident. Now that is tragic." She fanned through the previous month's pages and frowned.

"There's nothing in here about my mother. I thought—" She stopped in mid thought, her head whirling. "I saw her at Christmas," she said, a fragment of a memory teasing her. "She was upset with me." Her chest tightened. Alisa still didn't like the idea of displeasing her mother, but she was determined to get to the root of the recollection. "She was not happy that I broke off my engagement."

"Ah, the senator," he said. "I'm not surprised your mother wasn't pleased about the breakup."

"Why?"

Dylan remembered how appalled Alisa's mother had been when she'd caught him and Alisa kissing. He could tell the truth or he could be kind. Looking into Alisa's expectant gaze, he swallowed his resentment, or a portion of it, and opted for kind. "She always thought you deserved the very best. She was impressed by prestige and influence and she wanted that for you."

"Hmm," Alisa said, and snapped the datebook closed. "I didn't want him enough."

Dylan gave her a double take. "You wanna play that one again?"

She wiggled her shoulders. "I don't remember everything about the engagement, but I do remember that I broke up with him because I didn't love him enough to marry him." She sighed. "A shame," she said. "I have this sense that he was a nice guy." She pointed toward the hallway. "I want to see my bedroom."

Dylan tugged at his collar as he watched her whirl around the corner and wondered what was next. Her memories seemed to be returning at lightning speed. Anything could be next. His gut clenched. He could be next. Bracing himself, he slowly walked down the hall and glanced inside her bedroom.

Her closet door was flung open and she had two bureau drawers ajar as she rifled through them. His gaze, however, was snared by the decor. All the effort Alisa had not made to decorate the rest of the apartment had clearly gone into the bedroom. A four-poster brass bed dominated the room with a swirl of filmy white material looped around the top. The bedspread combined white and cream in the most luxurious silk he'd ever seen. A half dozen books were stacked on the nightstand next to a crystal lamp. He was curious about the titles.

His gaze kept turning back to the bed where several plump pillows were tossed casually atop the coverlet. He wondered what man may have shared that fantasy bed with Alisa and made some of her fantasies come true.

Something inside him growled at the thought. He took a deep breath and looked at Alisa. In one hand, she held a black silk teddy. In the other a pink satin chemise. He swallowed an oath. The contrast of the image of Alisa in the bad girl and lady lingerie was enough to make him sweat.

"Well, I'd say I like pretty things," she said more to herself than to him. "These are almost as good as billboards." She glanced up at Dylan, and her expression gradually turned self-conscious. She stuffed the lingerie back in the drawer and pushed it closed. "Well, that's probably enough for now," she said, standing. She smiled and clasped her hands together. "I think I must've just gotten started with the decorating. Who would have guessed?" she said, and walked from the room.

Dylan's gaze turned helplessly to the bed. It was all too easy to visualize Alisa spread on that bed wearing the black teddy or the pink chemise, or for that matter, nothing at all.

Dylan had known Alisa intimately when she was much younger. The image he'd stored of her all these years had been one of innocent passion. She had clearly grown up.

"Can we leave now?" she called back to him.

Dylan shook off the steamy images simmering in his mind. "Sure," he said, taking one last look at her bed and leaving the room.

Alisa's head was spinning with all the new information she'd gleaned about herself from her apartment. It was too much to assimilate at once, so she turned her attention to the breeze on her face as Dylan drove his Jaguar convertible back to his estate just outside St. Albans.

"Did visiting your apartment answer some of your questions?" he asked.

"Yes and no. Most of the time I felt as if I were visiting someone else's home."

"And your bedroom," he ventured.

She felt another wave of self-consciousness. Even though she couldn't remember decorating the room, Alisa felt protective of it. It was obviously a place where she indulged in sensual luxury. Her one extravagance in a life filled with practicality. "The bedroom raises questions, but that's for another day. After looking at my datebook, I've figured out why I've been a little difficult at times lately."

Dylan looked over at her at a stop sign, then gave a half grin as he accelerated. "Oh, really. I could've sworn you said you are not difficult."

Alisa fought a niggle of irritation. "I'm not. I mean, I'm sure I'm not difficult as a rule. I just might be a *little* difficult lately," she said, but didn't want to dwell on the fact. "The reason is I get tired of thinking and talking about me. It's so self-absorbing and well, depressing. I need to spend some time focusing on someone else." She smiled. "Today, that would be you."

He glanced at her with a combination of wary sexiness that made her wonder if he was still thinking about her bedroom. "How were you planning to focus on me?"

"Just a few questions," she said quickly. "You told me the story about how you didn't find out who your father was until he died and left you an inheritance, but I don't remember if you have any half brothers or half sisters."

"Two half brothers and one half sister, which in reality adds up to none," he said cynically.

"Why none?"

"Because nothing would make them happier than if I didn't exist. They do their best to disassociate themselves from me."

She shook her head. "I can see why it might be awkward, but it's not as if you're an ax murderer. You're not a dud. You're intelligent and talented. After they got over their initial discomfort, I would think they'd see you as 'the bonus brother.'"

"They're not over their initial discomfort," Dylan told her.

"How long have they known?"

"Six years," he said grimly.

Alisa looked at him and turned the unusual situation around in her head. "You've said what they want. What do you want?"

"What do you mean?"

"What do you want with your half brothers and half sister?"

"Nothing," he said with an apathy that rubbed at a tender place inside her. She sensed he'd learned that apathy from being disappointed.

"I would love to have brothers and sisters."

He shrugged. "In my case, blood isn't thicker than water. I'm not much for family ties. There's my mother, but that's always been an on-again, off-again thing."

"On-again, off-again?" she asked as he pulled into the long drive to his home.

"She's been married several times. Don't get me wrong. She's a nice lady, but her romantic relationships got in the way of having a normal life and being a single parent. I can't give her a normal life, but I bought a house for her where she can stay regardless of whatever man blows in or out of her life. Since I technically own it, it's safe from divorce proceedings."

Alisa absorbed his words and closed her eyes for a moment, searching her memory for a glimmer. None came. "I don't remember any of this about your mother."

"Yeah, well it's pretty forgettable. I never spent much time thinking about it."

Or talking about it, she suspected. "About your father," she began.

"I don't think about him at all," he said, his voice cold. "When I was a kid, I would've traded the world to know who my father was. When I finally found out who he was, he was dead. He might have been rich, but he was a coward. I'll take the money. My half siblings can have his name and everything that goes with it." He pulled the car to a hard stop next to the house and narrowed his eyes at her. "That covers everything about my so-called family," he said as he got out of the car and opened her door for her. "No fairy-tale endings."

The cold cynicism of his words chilled her. It was almost as if he were warning her. She saw a stubborn hopelessness in his eyes and something inside her rebelled at it. He emanated anger, justified anger, and she felt the oddest desire to defuse it at the same time that she knew she couldn't. Besides, he might as well have slammed the door in her face on the subject.

"I have an appointment in town," he said. "Do both of us a favor and take it easy this afternoon."

His directive took her by surprise. She felt her back stiffen. She didn't like being ordered, even if it was for her own good. "Thank you for your concern, and for taking me to my apartment," she said, and walked toward the house.

"Alisa, don't overdo it," he warned, his tone serious.

"Don't give me orders," she tossed back. "That may have worked when I was a little girl when I had a hard case of hero worship, but it doesn't work n—"

He was by her side and taking her arm before she could finish. It occurred to her that there were times she liked his height and times she didn't. This time she didn't. "This isn't about hero worship," he told her, his eyes glinting with anger. "I'm responsible for you."

"I don't need a baby-sitter or a nurse anymore."

"Then act like it," he said, and turned back toward the car.

Alisa fumed as she watched him get back in his car and pull out of the driveway. What a chauvinistic, heavy-handed jerk! She fought the undignified urge to stick her tongue out at him and yell, *bite me*. What made it worse was that he was right.

Pushing Dylan from her mind, Alisa went inside, fixed herself some lemonade and enjoyed a brief conversation with Dylan's housekeeper/cook, Mrs. Abernathy, a shy, but kind woman in her sixties. After lying down for a nap that wouldn't come, she rose and decided to explore the estate. From Mrs. Abernathy she'd learned a stable with horses was on the far west corner of the pasture.

The walk through his rolling fields stretched her a

little more than she'd expected, but the sight of a pony, a chestnut mare and a gelding rewarded her.

"Hello, beauties," she said as she walked in front of the stalls.

"Good-natured, too," a sturdy gray-haired woman said as she left the pony's stall. "I'm Meg Winters. Dylan lets me keep the horses here for classes for handicapped children."

"Really?" Alisa said, amazed. "He didn't tell me about this."

"I'm not surprised," Meg said. "It doesn't go with his image."

Alisa nodded slowly. "Wealthy, indifferent, materialistic, doesn't need anything from anybody," she said, stopping when she heard her voice rising with emotion.

"How long have you known him?" Meg asked curiously.

"About twenty years." Alisa introduced herself. "I'm a guest. I'm recovering from a too-long stay in the hospital. But I come bearing gifts," she said, pulling apples from her small backpack.

Meg nodded in approval. "Go ahead. Do you ride?"

Alisa visualized herself on the back of a horse. "Yes," she said. "But it's been a while."

"In that case, Sir Galahad would be a good choice. He's well broken, well behaved and pretty much does all the work for you. If you want to take him for a ride, he's your man." She cocked her head toward the door. "I'm headed home. Nice to meet you"

"And you," Alisa said and turned to offer an apple to the pony. She petted him and fussed over him, then meandered to the next stall which housed Sir Galahad. He took the apple from her palm with only his lips. "What a gentleman," she said, breathing in the scent of the clean barn and the horses. A lovely peace settled inside her as she stroked the horse. Her edginess and frustration seemed to drift away. It was a sweet temporary relief that her amnesia didn't matter to Sir Galahad, she thought with a sigh. Maybe a ride would do her good.

Dylan got a creepy feeling down the back of his spine when he searched the house for Alisa and didn't find her. The rain poured, thunder rolled, and dinner beckoned. He asked Ms. Abernathy if she knew where Alisa was.

"I'm sorry. The last time I saw her she was walking beyond the pool." The woman frowned. "She did seem interested in the horses when I told her about them earlier today."

His gut clenched. He glanced outside at the pouring rain. Surely she wouldn't go horseback riding after he expressly told her to take it easy? Dylan felt the beginning of a headache. He'd clearly had no idea what he was getting into when he'd offered to allow Alisa to recover at his home. At this rate, watching over her would be the death of him.

Swearing under his breath, he grabbed a rain poncho from the hall closet and stomped out of the house. With the rain coming down in sheets, he ran toward the horse pasture. Seeing no sign of her, he felt his tension crank another notch tighter. He swung open the barn door and heard her gasp.

"Dylan!" She lifted her hand to her throat. "What are you doing out in this rain?"

He took a deep breath and waited for his rush of relief to reach his heart. "Making sure you're okay," he finally said.

She shrugged. "I'm fine. I'm dry, I've got Sir Galahad for company and my water bottle. What else do I need?" She watched the water dripping from his poncho, then her gaze met his. "Were you worried?"

"I told you that I'm responsible for you," he said crossing his arms over his chest. "I didn't know if you'd decided to do something stupid like go horseback riding during a thunderstorm."

She lifted her chin. "Horseback riding during a thunderstorm," she echoed. "You must be confused. I'm not crazy, Dylan. I have amnesia."

"You also overdid it yesterday, had a nightmare last night and argued with me about taking it easy today."

She waved her hand in a dismissive gesture. "Anyone who wasn't a wuss would have argued with you today. You were incredibly *difficult* and you didn't even have the excuse of amnesia."

Plagued by thoughts of her smart mouth and fantasy bed all afternoon, Dylan again thought of how he'd like to put her mouth to work on him in a much more satisfying way than talking.

"I love this horse. Sir Galahad. Such a gentleman," she said, rubbing the animal's neck, then turning back to glance at Dylan. "Unlike his owner."

"He's also a gelding," Dylan informed her. "Unlike his owner."

She ignored his warning and walked toward him. "I must confess I'm confused. Meg told me you allow her to hold riding classes for handicapped kids. So tell me the truth Dylan, are you an arrogant, heartless, materialistic millionaire? Or do you just like to keep the fact that you have a heart a secret?" she asked pointing a finger at his chest. "And maybe you give a damn after all?"

The combination of the last month of waiting for Alisa to get better, his struggle not to care that her interest in him would soon turn to disdain, the steamy memory of her bedroom, and her smart sexy mouth pushed him over the edge.

His gaze holding hers, he backed her against a beam. "Yeah," he said. "Maybe I do give a damn."

Three

Alisa's heart hammered in her chest. *Oh, wow,* she thought, looking into a gaze that promised to eat her alive. Dylan was riding the razor's edge of control, and heaven help her, she liked that she had put him there. Forbidden excitement shot through her like adrenaline. Her mouth went dry and she tried to swallow.

He deliberately lowered his head inch by excruciating inch. The anticipation was delicious torture. She felt his gaze on her lips, then his mouth took hers. With a confidence that shook hers, he consumed her. His lips caressed and conquered in a kiss that felt like sex.

Her knees grew weak. His tongue slid inside her

mouth, and Alisa felt a sensual weakness suffuse her. She inhaled a quick shallow breath and the scent of rain and his aftershave filled her senses. His chest brushed her breasts, and he slid his hand to the back of her waist to draw her lower body against his. He was hard with arousal.

Alisa couldn't withhold a gasp. He deepened the kiss again, grinding himself against her, then pulling his mouth from hers. "Damn you, you're supposed to be taking naps and lying by the pool, not driving me nuts."

Alisa drew in a shaky breath, wishing for more starch in her knees and oxygen in her brain. She bit her lip at the power of her arousal and struggled for her equilibrium. "Well, the doctor did warn you I might be difficult," she finally managed in a voice husky to her own ears.

Dylan stared at her in disbelief, then dipped his head and swore.

"I can't help wondering," she said. "Have you and I ever kissed before?"

"Yeah, but—"

"But what?"

"It's been a long time," he said, moving away from her.

Inexplicably bereft, she crossed her arms over her chest. "Oh, well then, I guess that blows my first theory."

He met her gaze. "First theory?"

She shrugged. "Well, it was a pretty intense kiss.

Spontaneous combustion,'' she said. Or nuclear fusion. ''I thought that it was maybe a monstrous build-up of curiosity and tension over a lot of years. Like, say twenty. But if we've kissed before...'' She frowned. ''If we've kissed before, why did we stop?''

''Stop what?''

''Kissing before?''

He raked his hand through his hair. ''Because you were fifteen, your mother got married and you moved away.''

Alisa searched her memory for one tantalizing crumb and came up empty. ''I don't remember,'' she said, and wished with all her heart that she did.

He met her gaze, and she saw a sweet nostalgia come and go in his eyes. He gently chucked her chin. ''That's okay. Some things are best forgotten.'' He dropped his hand, and his eyes grew serious. ''In the meantime if you get bored while you're trying to recover, read a book or turn on the TV instead of pushing my buttons.'' He cocked his head to one side as if listening. ''Sounds like most of the storm's gone. Maybe we can go back to the house now.''

Still thinking about the heat of their kiss and the fact that she and Dylan had been teenage sweethearts, she watched him open the door.

''Looks safe to me,'' he said, waving her toward him. ''Come on.''

Alisa left the barn with him and walked silently. As they drew close to the house, she looked at him curiously. "Are you saying you didn't like it?" she asked.

He glanced at her in confusion. "Like what?"

"Kissing me," she said, coming to a stop. "Are you saying you didn't like kissing me?"

He stopped and shot her an impatient glance. "No, but you're recovering from a serious accident, and even though you may not realize it," he said in a dark voice, "you're vulnerable. I'm not going to take advantage of you."

"This is so confusing. One minute you're the materialistic millionaire, the next you're allowing handicapped kids to have horseback riding lessons on your property. One minute you're kissing me like—" She faltered, unable to find a sufficient description.

His gaze was dark with an emotion she couldn't quite name. "Like what?"

She lifted her chin. "Like you wanted to be doing a lot more than kissing. The next minute you're brushing me off because of some sense of honor. Which one is the real Dylan Barrows?"

"All of the above," he said, and led the way into the house.

Alisa stared after him, filled with frustration and questions. Damn her lack of memory. There was so much she wanted to know about herself and Dylan. The more she was around him, the more questions she had. She couldn't help feeling like a shell of a woman, a faux human. Her skin, hair and body were pure human, but inside she felt empty. She might as well be missing a limb. More than anything she wanted this lost feeling to go away. More than anything she wanted to remember everything about her, about Dylan.

Dylan left the house soon after dinner. He could rest easy that Alisa wouldn't find any more trouble today. She'd nearly fallen asleep at the table. As he strode into O'Malley's Bar to meet Michael and Justin, he tried to leave his concerns for her behind.

"How's life in chicken pox land?" he asked Justin.

Justin made a face. "The twins are getting over it, but Emily came down with it today. The kids are hot and itchy, and the summer heat is just making it worse. But Amy's great. She lets them swim in the little plastic pool in the backyard for half the day. I'm trying to talk her into a weekend away after the scourge has left us."

"You're welcome to my condo in Belize," Dylan said.

"You bought one?" Justin said. "I thought you would choose one of the flashier spots."

Dylan shook his head, thinking he'd grown weary of frantic nightlife. What he craved more than anything now was peace. "I'm turning into a crusty old bachelor. I like an island breeze, Beliken beer and a nice sunset."

"Sounds good," Justin said. "Add Amy to that picture and it would work for me."

''Speaking of women,'' Michael said, looking at Dylan curiously. ''How's it going with Alisa?''

''She still doesn't remember much, and she's very frustrated. We visited her apartment today, and that seemed to help a little.'' He paused, leaning against the bar. ''She's more of a handful than I expected.''

''Alisa? She's the sweetest girl in Virginia,'' Michael said. ''Aside from Kate, of course,'' he added, referring to his wife.

Dylan shook his head, thinking of her sensual bedroom and the way she'd taunted him this afternoon. ''She's not the little cookie girl anymore.''

''What do you mean? She can't make chocolate chip cookies anymore?'' Justin asked in an appalled voice.

''I don't know if she remembers how to make the cookies or not. I'm just saying she is more than I expected.''

''Is that good or bad?'' Justin asked.

Dylan thought about the passionate way she'd responded to him and the way he'd wanted to take her right there in the barn. ''Both.''

As the bartender delivered their beers, Michael and Justin looked at each other in confusion. ''I can't tell whether she's coming on to you or spitting in your face.''

''Try both,'' Dylan said, and took a long swallow of beer. ''I can't take advantage of her, because she's still recovering.''

''Plus she's gonna hate you when she remembers,''

Justin reminded him. He shook his head in commiseration. "I don't envy you."

"Yeah, well it's not my job to seduce her or be seduced by her. It's my job to provide a place for her to recover and that's what I'm doing," Dylan said. *Even if it kills me.* "But enough about that. I wanted to let you know I'll be negotiating with Grant Remington soon about the bioengineering project."

"Grant Remington," Michael said. "Your half brother."

Dylan gave a dirty chuckle. "He'd probably punch you for saying that."

Michael lifted an eyebrow. "I'd say he's damn lucky."

"How?" Dylan asked. "For having his inheritance whittled down to accommodate his father's slipup?"

"For getting you as his brother. He's got money to burn."

He tasted the familiar bitterness and shrugged. "I really don't give a damn as long as I get what I want."

The three men fell silent, but the noise of the bar lessened the impact. Michael cleared his throat. "In the meantime Kate told me to invite all of you to the house for a barbecue next Friday."

"Works for me," Justin said. "All the chicken pox should be gone by then."

"Good," Michael said, then glanced at Dylan. "Alisa's invited, too."

Dylan struggled with mixed feelings. Despite the

fact that Alisa was a handful, he liked having her to himself. It gave him a false sense of security, he realized wryly and nodded at Michael. Alisa would learn the truth sometime. Nothing was forever. "I'll bring her if she's still speaking to me," he said, and lifted his beer in a salute.

Alisa turned her attention to regaining as much of her memory as she could. She tried her best not to think about Dylan, at least while she was awake. She'd started dreaming about him while she slept. Sensual dreams where he kissed her endlessly and aroused her to the brink of pleasure, but she always awakened before he thrust inside her and took them both over the edge. She also always awakened fully aroused. Alisa couldn't decide which was worse—the nightmares or the erotic dreams.

She hitched a ride to her apartment with Dylan in the mornings while he went into work, then he gave her a return ride home at lunchtime. The past few days she'd eaten her lunch late, so she wouldn't spend extra time with him. He was like a hot stove to her, his heat drew her, but she knew she could get burned. She had the sense that a woman could become fascinated with Dylan and forget that the man had a lot of closed doors. Although she found herself both emotionally and sexually seduced by him, Alisa didn't want to fall into a trap.

After an endless weekend of looking through photo albums, listening to CDs she'd found at her apartment and putting together small fragments of her history, she returned and crossed paths with Dylan as he was sorting his mail. "How's it going?" he asked.

"Fine," she said. "I'm down to thirty-minute naps in the afternoon."

"No more nightmares?"

She shook her head, wishing she could shake the other dreams that made it too hot for her to sleep. Spotting an ivory invitation of some sort on the floor, she bent to pick it up. "You dropped it," she said, scanning the invitation. "Cocktail party inviting the board of Remington Pharmaceuticals. Are you going?"

"Probably not," he said, and tossed her a careless smile. "It's on Thursday night. I think there's a Braves game."

Alisa rolled her eyes. "There's always a Braves game. Will some of your half siblings be there?"

"Probably. Why?" he asked, looking at her.

"Just curious," she said. "Have you ever met your half family in a social setting?"

"Not unless you consider the official reading of the will," he said with a chuckle.

Alisa couldn't help laughing with him. "Aren't you curious how they'd act in a less formal setting?"

"No."

"I am."

"Then maybe you should go."

"Okay," she said without missing a beat. "What time should we leave?"

"What's this 'we,' Tonto?"

A memory flashed through her. She stared at him. "You've said that to me before."

He paused. "Yeah. About a hundred times."

"Reruns of *The Lone Ranger* television series," she said, the vague recollection strengthening. "That's how I got you to teach me to catch."

"You would sneak me into your house to watch the reruns while your mom was taking care of dinner at the cafeteria. The Granger boys had one television in the community room that was always breaking."

"But my mother had a nice television. It was small but it always worked." She shook her head. "I was so scared my mother would catch us. When she finally did—"

"I had to peel a zillion potatoes and take out the cafeteria trash for a month," he said. "It could have been worse if the headmaster had found out."

"I begged her not to tell him," Alisa said, recalling pleading with her mother. "You didn't stop teaching me to catch," she remembered. "Why? I had lost my bribe appeal."

"I don't know," he said. "You always had this combination of being determined as hell but nice. Tough on yourself, but kind to others. You were a loyal little thing."

Just when she was ready to give up on Dylan, he provided her with a glimpse of herself that filled up some of her emptiness and gave her hope that she could recapture her past. Every day she struggled with how someone without a past could make a future.

Realizing she'd been distracted from their original conversation, she switched gears with a smile. "What time do I need to be ready for the cocktail party?" she asked.

"Never o'clock," he said, turning back to the mail.

"Hmm," she said, thinking. "Are you afraid of your half brothers and sister?"

He looked up at her with more firepower in his eyes than a twenty-one-gun salute. "You have to care about something to fear it," he told her in a too-calm voice.

"So there's nothing you want from them?" she asked, unable to fathom the possibility. She would have given her eyeteeth for a brother or sister. "Nothing at all?"

"Nothing," he said definitively, then paused and frowned. "Except..."

"Except what?"

He closed down. "It's business," he said.

Frustrated by the walls Dylan put up around himself, she sighed. Another childhood memory floated through her mind. He had always dared her to step a little further. "Well there's only one thing I can say at this point. I triple dare you to go to the cocktail party," she told him, drawing on the saying they'd used as children.

Dylan stared after her, taking in the sight of her backside as her taunting words reverberated in his mind. Irritated, vaguely seduced, he dismissed her dare. When they'd been kids, *he* had always been the one to dare her. Had the accident made her more adventurous? he wondered. Or perhaps she had become more adventurous since they'd parted company in college. For all the time he'd known Alisa, he'd lost a lot of growing time with her. The loss gnawed at him.

She wasn't nearly as acquiescent to him as she'd once been. She didn't look at him with hero worship in her eyes anymore. She looked at him with a woman's curiosity and fascination, and the change both unsettled and drew him. He was accustomed to women who were intent on his comfort and satisfaction. Alisa seemed more intent on knowing him and challenging him. Despite her current vulnerability, she'd grown much stronger during their years apart.

He thought about her dare again and swore under his breath. The notion of spending more than thirty seconds in the presence of his half siblings turned his stomach. However, the blond witch who'd invaded his house and thoughts had a point. He did want something from the Remingtons, and if showing up at a cocktail party could help him get what he wanted, he would do it.

Six-thirty, he'd told her, Alisa thought as she fanned through the closet in her apartment. Her mind was humming with thoughts of Dylan. He was im-

portant to her. No way around that fact. She didn't
understand it, and didn't have all the facts, but she
had a lot of feelings and intuition. She didn't know
why it was so important to her for him to gain some
sort of connection with his half brothers and sister.
Some might say it was none of her business, but she
had this strong gut feeling and she couldn't ignore it.
Alisa had learned that not having all her memories
and facts in place meant she needed to rely on her
gut.

She'd also figured out part of the reason he irritated
her. With the exception of the time he'd kissed her,
when Dylan looked at her, she felt as if he were seeing her as the little girl she'd once been. He was protective of her, and while she appreciated the senti-
ment, she didn't like the idea of being seen as the
goofy little girl who'd followed him around. The image didn't suit her at all. Alisa may not have a handle
on her past, but she believed she'd been a strong person, and if she hadn't been as strong as she wanted
to be before, she was darn well going to start now.

She found three black cocktail dresses and arranged
them on the bed to make a selection. None of them
wowed her. Returning to her closet, she fanned
through again, this time finding a dress wrapped in
plastic with the tag still attached. She lifted the plastic
and took a second and third look. She suspected the
dress was an impulse purchase and she'd been torn
as to whether to return it or not.

The white dress was a fitted, above-the-knee chemise in classic white. The only thing that prevented it from being a nice, regular dress, were the two horizontal slits in the material covering the chest, clearly designed to expose a hint of skin and cleavage. Wearing this dress, Alisa concluded, would require guts. It was not a little-girl dress.

She glanced at her choices and wondered why the clothing choice mirrored her dilemma with Dylan. The prudent choice would be one of the black dresses. The prudent choice with Dylan would be to let him continue to look at her as the little girl.

Alisa picked up the white dress and tossed prudence out the window.

Four

This was a bad idea, Dylan said to himself as he waited for Alisa in the foyer. He had a feeling Alisa saw the potential for a fairy-tale ending with his un-family, and she was in for a rude awakening. He wouldn't have agreed to go if her sexy little dare hadn't gotten under his skin.

He shook his head. No matter. They wouldn't stay long. He heard her footsteps on the stairs. "We're only going to be there fifteen minutes, tops," he warned as he turned around. "Most of the board members prefer quiet wine and quiet conversation, so don't expect—"

He broke off when he saw her. He didn't know what he'd expected, but he hadn't expected this. Her hair was pulled up in an unstructured bun and she wore very little makeup, just enough to make him keep looking at her mouth and eyes. Pearl earrings dangled from her earlobes, and what her dress didn't show was going to keep him up nights for the next month.

The slivers of golden skin the white dress revealed could have caused a riot. He'd never been tongue-tied with a woman, but he was close to it now.

She met his gaze. "Don't expect what?" she prompted him.

He adjusted his tie. "So don't expect too much excitement."

She paused for a long moment, still holding his gaze. "There's more than one kind of excitement."

Her eyes held a combination of daring and amusement that affected him like an intimate stroke. He walked behind her as she headed for the front door, his mind filled with sexual possibilities. He bit back an oath. This was going to be an even longer night than he'd anticipated.

After they drove into town, Dylan and Alisa climbed the steps to the St. Albans Fine Arts Museum. They entered through the heavy wooden doors, then took the elevator to the third floor where the reception was to be held. Dylan couldn't keep his eyes off Alisa. Quietly observing everything, she didn't seem to be the least bit aware that he'd thought about stripping her clothes off her at least twenty times during the past twenty minutes.

They walked through another set of doors only to be greeted by Kirsten Remington. Dylan watched his younger half sister's jaw drop nearly to the ground.

"Dylan Barrow," she said as though he were the scourge of the earth. "You weren't expected."

"Surprise," he said with a dry grin. "Kirsten Remington, this is Alisa Jennings."

Alisa extended her hand. "How nice to meet you," she said. "You'll have to excuse my lack of knowledge, but I'm not in the pharmaceutical business. You said Remington? Any relation to Archibald Remington?"

Kirsten lifted her chin. "Archibald Remington was my father."

Alisa nodded. "Oh," she said with a smile. "So you're Dylan's half sister."

Kirsten paled and seemed to have a hard time catching her breath. "Excuse me. My fiancé is waving at me."

"Torpedo one," Dylan said.

Alisa looked at him. "Why do you say that? She was polite."

"Uh-huh," he said in mock agreement. "I was just wondering if I would need smelling salts for her."

"It wasn't that bad," she insisted.

"Alisa," he told her, "they don't like to be reminded that they're related to me."

"Tough," she said, with an indomitable attitude.

''Introduce me to your work buddies,'' she said with a smile. ''Show me a good time.

He guided her around the room, introducing her to the members of the board. Although each board member appeared surprised by his presence, Alisa somehow managed to get past their reserve. Finally he and Alisa approached Grant, who was holding court at the other end of the room. Grant looked at him, but might as well have looked right through him. For some reason tonight it didn't bother him.

As soon as Grant finished talking, Dylan walked directly in front of the man. ''How are you tonight, Grant?''

Surprise glinted in the man's eyes. ''Fine, and you? We're surprised you attended, since you've never come before.''

''Change can be good,'' Dylan said.

''Some change,'' Grant said.

''Grant Remington, I'd like you to meet Alisa Jennings.''

Grant nodded and murmured a pleasantry.

''Another Remington,'' Alisa said with a smile. ''Half brother?''

Grant went perfectly still. His nostrils thinned as he took a quick breath. ''I hadn't thought of that.''

''Really?'' she said brightly. ''It occurred to me how lucky all of you are.''

Grant swallowed. ''All of who?''

''Well, you and Dylan and your sister and your other brother. What's his name?''

"Walter," he said, looking at Alisa in confusion. "Lucky?" he echoed.

"Yes," she said. "Think about it. You could have ended up with an ax murderer or some subintelligent bum for a brother. Instead you got an extremely intelligent, motivated man who's an asset to the company."

Dylan squeezed her hand to signal her to stop.

Grant flexed his jaw. "Is that so?"

"Yes, it is," she said. "But Dylan tells me you're a smart man, so I'm sure you already know that. And in Dylan's case, he got lucky because he could have ended up with two brothers and a sister who were so insecure they couldn't see the good in him. Instead he got you," she said.

Dylan was going to kill her.

Grant gave a smile that didn't reach his eyes. "How kind of you to point all of this out to me. Now, if you'll excuse me."

"Torpedo two. Time for us to go," Dylan said, shaking his head and guiding her from the room. He didn't trust himself to speak, and she must have sensed it since she didn't say a word on the drive home.

As soon as they entered the front door, he rounded on her. "Why in hell did you do that?"

She shook her head as if she were unable to explain it. "I don't know. I probably need to talk to the hospital shrink about it."

"What?" Dylan asked.

"I don't know," she said, wincing. "It must go back to our childhood. I have this overwhelming urge to protect you."

Dylan stared at her. "Do I look like I need protecting?"

"No," she admitted, taking in the length of him in a way that told him she was very aware of him as a man. "But the longer we were there, the more upset I got about the situation. It should be different."

"Lots of things should be different," he said with more than a trace of impatience "That doesn't mean they are."

"Maybe things aren't different because nobody does or says anything to change matters."

"This is none of your business."

"I know," she agreed wholeheartedly. "But this is wrong and someone needed to say something."

"And it had to be you."

She stared at him a long moment, then shook her head. "I don't know what made me do it. It isn't rational. Maybe there's some kind of weird karma thing going on."

"Weird karma?" he echoed. Heaven help him.

"I feel like I owe you."

Her statement blew him away. He took a breath to clear his head. "Because I'm letting you recover at my house."

She frowned, shaking her head. "It goes back further than that. I just have this feeling that you did something so special or so important to me that I owe you.''

Dylan immediately remembered how he had hurt her during college, and his stomach dropped. ''You don't owe me,'' he assured her. ''You've never owed me,'' he said, and left her staring after him. He had to escape her searching gaze. He had to escape his own disgust with himself.

Alisa felt incredibly foolish. After donning a nightgown, she'd tossed in bed for more than an hour, then given up. She should be tired. She'd certainly had a doozy of an evening.

Even though she'd defended him, Dylan was justified in being angry with her. It was none of her business if he and his half siblings wasted their entire lives avoiding each other. Dylan was more than man enough to defend himself. She had the sense that he'd protected her more than once during her growing-up years.

Upset by her thoughts, she pushed open the French doors to the balcony and walked outside into the warm night air. Closing her eyes, she lifted her face and bathed in the gentle light of the moon. She wondered when she would sleep through the night again. If she wasn't dreaming of Dylan, she was pushing her brain for more information on her past.

Why did she care so much for him, when he set solid boundaries against her? She wondered if he'd been a quasibrother figure for her, but then remembered they'd been teenage sweethearts. She wondered if they'd been lovers. Her skin heated with the possibility. That might explain the connection she felt with him.

A delicious breeze stirred the air. Alisa savored it, and a decadent thought flitted across her mind. The breeze whispered over her again, and she wished she could feel the air over her body, her bare body.

Frustration bubbled in her throat and she walked to the outer wall of the balcony, lifting her head to the breeze. Alisa suspected she'd been modest before. Certainly she wasn't the kind of woman to strip off her clothes on a balcony just to feel the breeze. But perhaps, she thought, she'd secretly wanted to do that. She wondered if beneath her white-bread exterior beat a passionate, adventurous heart.

Standing in the darkness of his room, Dylan watched her glance from side to side, then he held his breath as she lifted the straps of her gown and slid the silky garment down her body. She didn't know he watched her, and he had the vague feeling of being a voyeur, but he couldn't have turned away if he'd tried.

The moonlight poured over her curves like cream. She lifted her hair off the back of her neck, causing her back to arch and her breasts to thrust forward, the tips like berries. The balcony wall hid her lower body from his sight, but Dylan remembered. He remembered a night when he'd burned and made her burn, too.

She'd danced with him at the fraternity party. There'd been plenty of beer available, but he and Alisa had been getting drunk on each other. After rediscovering each other, they'd spent every available moment together. That night, when they'd danced, they'd chosen a dark spot near the corner of the room and rubbed their bodies against each other.

He had seemed unable to stop kissing her, and she hadn't seemed to want him to stop. He'd been so hard he'd been aching with it. He'd taken her away from the party to a secluded area off campus where they'd necked on a blanket with the stars shining around them.

Dylan hadn't spent much time looking at the stars. He'd been too hungry for Alisa. Even now he could remember the sounds of their breaths in the fall night air. He'd touched her breasts, and her soft moan had driven him crazy. Tugging her blouse loose, he'd inhaled the sweet scent between her breasts and kissed the creamy tips. When he'd felt her shudder, he'd taken a deep breath.

"I can't get close enough," he'd said. "But you're probably freezing."

"I'm not cold at all," she'd told him, lifting her hand to his cheek. "I can't get close enough to you, either."

He'd pulled off his shirt and pressed his chest against her breasts. The sensation was indescribable.

He'd known she was inexperienced, but he'd felt as if he'd wanted her for a lifetime. Being with Alisa made him feel safe. Being inside her would make him whole. He kissed her again and slid his hand beneath her skirt and panties to find her wet with arousal. He stroked the petals of her femininity and prepared her by sliding his finger inside her.

Her hands were restless over his chest and shoulders. He guided them down to where he ached. He opened his jeans for her and she fondled him with an awkward tenderness that made him feel as if he would burst.

His urgency drove him. He slid her skirt down, and her skin was pale in the moonlight, her thighs creamy in invitation.

She looked at him, her gaze full of passion and a tinge of apprehension he could tell she was trying to hide. "I've never—"

He covered her lips with his fingers. "I know," he said. "I'll protect you," he promised, and he had.

He thrust inside her and caught her gasp with his lips. She felt like wet velvet surrounding him, milking him. He looked into her eyes of pure love, and Dylan had known where he belonged.

Dylan's body pulsed with the memory of making love to Alisa. He watched her touch her bare arm and the top of her breast. His mouth went dry. His heart tightened in his chest at the memory of how she'd gone into battle for him tonight. He had lost so much when he'd lost her all those years ago, far more than he ever would have imagined. Even if he had her back for a while, she would eventually leave him again when she regained her memory. Dylan had learned the hard way that nothing lasts forever. This was no different.

The following morning, Alisa rode to her apartment with Dylan again. After an hour of prowling around her apartment, however, she grew restless. In her datebook she'd seen a notation for Granger one afternoon every week. Her doctor hadn't released her yet to drive, so she called a taxi and followed her nose to Granger.

She felt totally at ease with the layout of Granger and easily remembered the location of the cafeteria and the cottage where she'd spent her childhood years. She saw a group of boys playing baseball and remembered taking her own turn at bat. In many of her childhood memories Dylan's presence was woven like a strong bright-red thread in a tapestry.

She even remembered why she'd visited Granger once a week before the clerk in the office reminded her. "Sorry I'm late, Ms. Henderson," Alisa said, so pleased she'd remembered the woman's name without a prompt she could have wept.

Gladys Henderson glanced up from her desk and gave a cry of delight. She swept around the counter with surprising speed for her girth and gave Alisa a big hug. "What a sight for sore eyes! We've been worried about you. I visited you in the hospital that first week, but you were out of it.'' She lifted Alisa's arms to the sides and surveyed her. ''You look beautiful. How's your brain, sweetheart?''

Alisa laughed at the woman's warmth and bluntness. ''I have some gaps, but I remember how to read, and I remember that Robbie and I were working on *The Lion, the Witch and the Wardrobe* by C. S. Lewis.''

Ms. Henderson smiled. ''Then you're doing pretty good. He missed you something terrible. Let me see if I can find him,'' she said, heading back for the phone. She called the dorm manager and told him to send Robbie to the office. Alisa chatted with Ms. Henderson while they waited.

Robbie, a thin, young-looking ten-year-old, walked into the office with an expectant expression on his face. As soon as he saw Alisa, he smiled, revealing a missing tooth.

''Robbie!'' she said, rushing toward him and embracing him. ''One of your teeth is gone.''

''It finally fell out,'' he said. ''Two years later than everyone else. How is your head? They told me you hurt it very bad.''

Alisa nodded. ''I did, but I'm much better now. How much reading have you been doing?''

Robbie stuffed his hands in his pockets and shifted from foot to foot. ''I read a whole chapter, but it was hard.''

Alisa smiled. ''Would you like to start reading together again?''

His face lit up. "Oh, yeah. It's a lot more fun with you."

"Next week. Wednesday at three o'clock," she said, remembering their standing appointment.

He gave a thumbs-up and nodded. "I'm glad you're okay."

"Me, too," she said, and felt somewhat lighter. The world suddenly made a little more sense to her.

Dylan counted to ten, then twenty, then one hundred when he couldn't find Alisa at her apartment at their agreed-upon meeting time. There was no reason to call the police, he told himself even as he felt a trickle of perspiration stream down his back.

He doubted he would ever get that call from the hospital out of his head. They hadn't been sure she would make it and even though Alisa couldn't stand him, he didn't want to imagine a world without her. He'd never been much for praying, but he'd spent the next several days in long conversation with the Almighty.

He checked his watch again and racked his brain for where she might have gone. He spied a taxi round the corner and pull into the parking lot and exhaled in relief as Alisa exited the cab and looked for him. He tightened his hands around the steering wheel several times to relieve his tension, then got out of the car.

"There you are," she called, and walked toward him. Her face was shining with such joy that he couldn't call her attention to the time. "I remember," she said, and hugged him.

Confused, Dylan felt a mixture of happiness and foreboding. He automatically closed his arms around her. She couldn't possibly remember everything, could she?

"I remember Mrs. Henderson at Granger's and I remember Robbie is a little boy I've been helping with reading. And I remember the total layout of the Granger campus." She looked up at him, her eyes filled with tears. "I remembered Mrs. Henderson's name before she told me, and I even remembered the name of the book Robbie and I were reading together."

Her joy was contagious. He'd watched her struggle from the very beginning. "What do you want to do now?"

"I want to make chocolate chip cookies," she said with a knowing glance. "My mother's recipe," she added with determination. "And I want to see if I can do it from memory."

His heart contracted. "What do you remember about your mother's cookies?"

"I used to snitch a few and give them to some of the guys."

"You were the cookie girl, and everyone always wanted your cookies."

She paused for a moment, then looked up at him from the veil of her eyelashes. "Did you always want my cookies?"

Five

——

"**T**hey're still missing something," Alisa said with a frown after the third batch.

"Taste great to me," he said, having eaten entirely too many cookies. "At this rate we won't have any room for the barbecue at Michael's house tonight."

She glanced at him and winced. "I forgot. Since Michael and Justin were Granger boys, too, maybe they can tell me what's wrong with them."

"Nothing is wrong with these cookies," Dylan said emphatically.

"I still think there's something missing." She glanced at the clock. "What time do we need to leave?"

"Fifteen minutes," he said, not all that eager to go

to the barbecue tonight. Who knew what she would remember next? "We don't have to go if you're too tired or too full," he casually offered.

She shook her head. "Oh, no. I want to see what else I remember. This could be fun."

Yes, he thought. Or not.

Thirty minutes later he drew near the turnoff for Michael's home. Alisa glanced at him. "My cookies didn't make you sick, did they? You've been very quiet."

"No. I've just got a few things on my mind."

He seemed so distant, Alisa thought, and wished things were different. She wished a lot of things that made her heart hurt. She had the strongest yearning to be the one he felt he could turn to, but she knew she wasn't. The knowledge hurt a tender spot deep inside her.

He pulled to a stop, and she covered his hand with hers. "I hope all those things work out," she said, reaching out to him the best way she knew.

He met her gaze and in his eyes she saw a kaleidoscope of emotions. The one that affected her most profoundly was regret. "Some will," he said, "and some won't."

Alisa's heart twisted. She sensed that he was certain something important to him would not work out.

He glanced up. "Here they come. Do you want me to give you names or—"

"No! Let me guess. I'm getting more and more of my memory back. Let me see what I remember." She got out of the car and was immediately greeted by twin boys, pre-school age, and a girl, slightly older, followed by two couples. Her memory creaked like a rusty wheel. "I did some baby-sitting for you," she said.

The twins gave big nods. "And you let us eat cookies," one of them said.

"For dinner," the other one added.

The little girl covered her mouth and made a shushing sound. "You weren't supposed to tell!"

"Starts with a *J*," Alisa murmured.

"Jeremy," one of the twins said proudly. "I'm Jeremy and I start with a *J*. Aunt Amy told me."

Alisa laughed and tried to concentrate. "Emily."

Emily's eyes lit up and she nodded with a huge smile. She mouthed the letter *N*.

The cue did the trick. "Nick," she said, delighted with herself.

He nodded and stepped closer to her. He pointed his finger at her head. "You bonked your head. Are you all better?"

"Mostly better."

"Can you still bake cookies?"

She heard Dylan's muffled chuckle and smiled. "I brought some cookies with me and I need someone to tell me if I baked them correctly."

The twins jumped up and down. "Me! Me! Me!"

"After dinner," a red-haired woman said, then turned to Alisa. "No more guessing games. Save your brain strain for something more important. I'm Amy, Justin's wife.''

Alisa immediately liked the woman all over again. ''Thanks,'' she said and glanced at Justin. ''How's the market?''

He blinked in surprise. ''Hey I saw you in the hospital and you didn't remember squat. You're remembering everything.''

''Breakthrough day,'' she said, riding the wave. She looked at her hosts. ''Michael and Kate, it's nice of you to invite me.''

Both Michael and Kate embraced her. ''We're so glad you're okay,'' Kate said sincerely.

Overwhelmed with emotion at finding another part of herself that had been lost, Alisa struggled with tears. Floundering, she instinctively looked for Dylan.

Correctly reading her face, he put his arm at her back. ''I need some help with these cookies,'' he said, taking the pressure off Alisa. ''How soon can we have those burgers?''

The kids clamored for the cookies, and the group scattered.

''Thanks,'' she whispered.

''No problem. Remember, you're recovering.''

''Nice way of saying I'm difficult?'' she asked wryly.

''I did not use the 'D' word,'' he said firmly.

''You know everything that has happened to me since the accident has been a roller-coaster ride. I don't understand why you've stuck with it.''

His gaze held hers. "I have my reasons."

She would love to know what those reasons were, but she wouldn't be finding out tonight, she realized as they neared a long picnic table. Alisa enjoyed a lighthearted hour with the adults and children. Kate and Amy made her feel at ease and brought her up to speed on recent events in their families.

"The adoption has been official for several weeks now," Amy said. "Justin has been great for all of us."

"Who would have known," Kate said, "that our allergic-to-marriage-tightwad-millionaire could be such a great instant dad?"

"He was a good guy when he was a kid," Alisa said.

Amy raised her eyebrows and exchanged a glance with Kate. "You remember back that far?"

"I remember some," Alisa said. "I remember my childhood, but it gets sketchy during my teen years. Very recent memories are starting to come back. I wish I remembered more about Dylan. He's done so much for me since the accident, but I can hardly recall anything about him after I was about twelve years old. I just have all these feelings I can't explain."

Turning silent, Kate and Amy looked at her with concern. Kate sat down beside Alisa and gave her a quick squeeze. "You've been through a lot. Give yourself time. No matter what you remember or don't remember, there are people who care for you deeply, and we're all relieved that you're getting better. And if you need anything at all, you are to call me."

"Or me," Amy said.

Alisa sighed, taking comfort in Kate's words and the support both women offered her. At the same time, however, she knew she wouldn't rest until her memory filled in some very important gaps.

Nick and Jeremy raced to stand in front of her. Cookie crumbs dotted their chins. "So far, we think the cookies are good," Nick said.

"But we need to eat some more to make sure," Jeremy said with a craftiness beyond his four years.

Amy intervened. "How many cookies have you eaten?"

"Not many," Jeremy said.

Emily walked up behind them. "Four cookies each," she said.

The boys glared at her.

"You've had enough. I don't want you getting sick in Justin's car again." She winced in Alisa's direction. "The joys of fatherhood."

Alisa glanced at Justin. Her attention naturally shifted to the man beside him—Dylan. She wondered what his children would look like. She wondered what kind of father he might be. She wondered what kind of wife he might choose, and immediately felt a twist of something very close to envy. Uncomfortable with the direction of her thoughts, she turned her attention to Amy and her children. "Feel free to take some cookies home."

Dylan strolled to her side and whispered in her ear, "See, I told you all the boys want your cookies."

His playful, seductive tone heated her blood. "You never answered me. Does that include you?"

Dylan paused. "Sometimes we want what we can't have."

She felt a dart of impatience. "Why does this sound like forbidden cookies?"

Later that night Alisa dreamed of Dylan again. He kissed her lips and touched her body. His arousal made her burn. She wanted more, so much more. She wanted him closer than close. He touched her intimately and just as she drew close to ecstasy, his image faded.

"No! Don't go!" she yelled, waking herself. She sat up breathing heavily, her breasts heavy with arousal, her skin warm, and between her legs she was swollen with need.

Frustrated beyond belief, she tossed off her covers and could not withhold a shriek. She would have preferred to scream at the top of her lungs, but she didn't want to wake Dylan.

Forgoing the lamp on her bedside table for cool air, she padded across the floor to the balcony and threw open the French doors.

A second passed before Dylan burst into her room. "What's wrong? Another bad dream?"

She glared at the cause of her restless nights. His bare chest gleamed in the moonlight, his black slacks had been hastily drawn on. They were unbuttoned. She suspected he was naked beneath them. "In a manner of speaking," she said.

He stepped closer and touched her face. "Your skin is warm. Are you sick?"

"Probably," Alisa said with irony and tilted her head away from him. "I'm fine," she said, crossing her arms over her chest and looking away from him. "You can go back to bed."

"What's going on?"

She was unbearably frustrated. What did she have to lose by telling the truth? "I've been having bad dreams about you," she said.

"Bad? How?"

She paused a second, then shrugged. "Erotic dreams."

A long, thick silence followed. "Oh."

"I keep dreaming you're kissing me and making love to me, and we get closer and closer. Just when I want you most, you fade away." She took a breath and closed her eyes, willing her heart rate to slow. "Why do I keep dreaming about you? Why are you so important? What were we before my accident?" she asked, opening her eyes and turning to face him.

"Our relationship was complicated."

"How?" she asked, drowning in his dark eyes. "Tell me," she whispered, moving so close to him she could feel the heat of his body. "Show me."

His eyes narrowed, then it was as if something inside ripped. He slid his hand through her hair and drew her mouth to his. He devoured her as if he'd wanted her for a very long time, as if she were a need long denied. She felt plundered and seduced, immediately, fully aroused.

"You make it difficult for me to do the right thing," he muttered against her mouth.

"I'm not sure we agree on what the right thing is," she said, and pulled his mouth to hers again. She tasted his dark, masculine flavor and was filled with the familiar desire for more.

He pulled back slightly and rubbed his hands over her shoulders, pushing one of the straps of her chemise down over her shoulder. "I saw you when you were naked on the balcony. I didn't sleep the rest of the night."

"That's fair," she said breathlessly, holding his gaze. "You've been keeping me awake."

A flame lit in his eyes and with one finger, he dragged the other strap of her chemise down. She held her breath as he slid his index finger down over her chest to the swell of her breast, then deliberately lower over her nipple. The silky chemise fell to her waist, baring her breasts to his gaze.

She felt him drink in the sight of her as he slid his finger around her nipple in a circular motion. Alisa inhaled a shaky breath that drew his attention to her face. He backed her against the wall and meshed his chest with her breasts. Alisa sighed at the exquisite sensation.

French kissing her, he slid his hands down to her

hips and guided her against his hardness. He stepped between her thighs and rocked intimately against the cradle of her femininity.

He made a low moan of pleasure that vibrated throughout her and dipped his head to taste the hardened tips of her breasts. Leaning her head helplessly back against the wall, Alisa felt the roar of arousal in her blood and let it take her higher and higher.

She felt the cool night air on her bare legs, then his thighs intertwined with hers. His touch felt new and somehow not new. It was as if he knew her body. How? she wondered.

His fingers slid beneath her panties, and she gasped in surprise.

''You feel so good,'' he told her, finding her sensitive pleasure point. ''Like velvet.''

Alisa wanted more. She wanted to feel him inside her. She wanted him as out of control as she felt. She opened her mouth, but his stroking fingers stole her words. Plunging a finger inside her, he rubbed her bead of sensitivity with his thumb. With each stroke, the coil inside her tightened. Heat suffused her, and a spasm of pleasure ripped through her.

She shuddered against him as the aftershocks of his touch shook her. Inhaling deeply, she clung to him, overwhelmingly aware of his unspent passion. His arousal was more than a body part; it was so powerful it permeated the air she breathed. ''I didn't want it to be that way,'' she told him in a low voice. ''I wanted you—''

"—you're not ready," he said flatly. "You're still recovering."

On the heels of their intimacy, his tone jarred her. "I think I'm the better judge of that."

Silence followed, and his disagreement hung between them. It hardly seemed possible, but Alisa felt shut out and rejected, and it hurt. "Why did you kiss me and touch me?"

"You needed the release," he said in a low voice. "I could give you that."

"So it was like a favor?" she asked, feeling her heart contract painfully. Humiliation trickled in like acid. She stepped back and pulled her gown up to cover herself.

He reached for her, but she stepped back. "It wasn't a favor. You could feel my response."

She shook her head in confusion. "I don't understand this."

"I told you you're not ready."

"I don't buy that," she said. "I wanted you and you held back. Did I hurt you and I don't remember it? Did I betray you in some way?"

He stiffened as if she'd struck him. "No, but I know you wouldn't forgive me for taking advantage of you."

"You wouldn't have been taking advantage of me. I made it perfectly clear that I wanted you." She shook her head again. "The only thing you've done is totally confuse me. I didn't want a favor. I have all these feelings for you and I don't know where they come from. They're so strong I don't know what to do with them. I wanted to make love to you. I wanted to be your lover and for you to be mine. This was about more than release. Don't do me any more favors. I can turn on the cold water in the shower just as easily as the next person," she said, and left him on the balcony.

Walking directly to the bathroom, she closed the door behind her and stripped. She turned on the cold water and stepped under the punishing, chilly spray. She needed to wash Dylan out of her head and body. She just wasn't sure a cold shower would get him out of her soul.

Dylan spent the night restlessly pacing his bedroom. His aroused body quarreled with his sense of honor. Why hadn't he taken Alisa when he could have? She had wanted him. Why was he denying himself and her?

The answer came immediately. Her memory would return sometime. The impending knowledge hung over his head like the blade of a guillotine, poised to fall at any minute. Alisa would remember the betrayal. Worse for Dylan, she would remember her disillusionment with him.

Even having the certainty of her waning feelings staring him in the face, he hated that his denial had hurt her. Her doctor had told him not to rush any traumatic memories. Alisa had enough to deal with by facing each day, one day at a time.

Dylan knew his purpose was to help her heal. That was where he had to keep his focus.

The following morning Alisa came downstairs, but didn't sit down to join him for breakfast. Her gaze was tumultuous. Frustration and confusion warred for domination on her features. Dylan stood.

She folded her hands in front of her. "I think it might be best for me to go back to staying at my apartment. I remember French, so I can also go back to work...."

"Your doctor still hasn't released you," he told her, feeling his gut twist.

"He will soon, especially if I press him," she countered.

"One more week," Dylan suggested. "You can try going to work half days. Stay here and I'll take you."

"Why?"

"Because I feel responsible for you," he told her.

"That's getting old."

"Okay, then you owe me," he said, ruthlessly taking another tack. "I brought you here to take care of you. In exchange I want you to remain here one more week and be hostess when I invite my pseudo siblings for dinner."

Six

Alisa gaped at Dylan in surprise. She knew he joked about many things, but his sense of humor seemed to abandon him when it came to the subject of family. Despite her humiliation over last night, she couldn't help feeling strangely honored that he would include her in anything involving his father's children. "Did I hear you correctly? You want me to stay another week to help plan a dinner with your half brothers and sister? I thought you couldn't stand them."

He shook his head. "There's a difference between active dislike and apathy. Don't mistake this as an opportunity for a big emotional reunion."

"Then why are you inviting them?"

He exhaled and hesitated a long moment. "There's

something I want, and it will be easier to get it if I have their cooperation.''

Business, Alisa concluded, and felt a trickle of disappointment. She couldn't help thinking that if Dylan and his father's children got acquainted, they would all be the richer for it. She could see, however, from Dylan's stony expression that he had that door of possibility locked tighter than Fort Knox. Much like his heart.

''You look disappointed,'' he said. ''You need to get over this notion of happy endings. They just don't happen every time.''

''I know they don't happen every time,'' Alisa said. ''But if I give up on the possibility, then I'll be cynical and unhappy like you. It may sound crazy, but I think hope is magic.'' She lifted her chin at the glimmer of disbelief in his eyes and pointed her index finger gently at his chest. ''Besides, I think you hope for more than you admit. Otherwise, why would you have spent so much time hoping for me to regain consciousness when the doctors said my chances weren't very good?''

''That was different. It was a matter of life and death.'' He closed his hand around her finger and lifted it to his lips. ''And I know the world is a better place if you're here.'' He gave a wry smile and gently nipped her fingertip. ''I'm not a total heartless cynic.''

Her heart raced at the combination of his touch and the intent expression in his eyes. She knew he wasn't a total heartless cynic. That was a big part of her problem. He would be so much easier to dismiss if he were. Instead she got glimpses of the heart of Dylan that made her want more and more of him.

"Will you stay?" he asked.

Alisa tried to picture herself refusing Dylan and walking away, but she couldn't. After all he had done for her, refusing him wasn't possible.

"One week," she said, pulling her finger from his lips. She had the strange sensation that she'd just agreed to a week-long emotional roller-coaster ride. How, she wondered, was she going to make herself stop wanting more of him?

The first couple of days, with the exception of riding to work with him in his car, she stayed away from Dylan. She planned the menu for the dinner with the housekeeper and sent written invitations to the addresses Dylan had given her. During the short commute, however, she was sensitive to his closeness. His scent stirred her, and she often felt him watching her. Alisa always had the sense that there was a caldron beneath his seemingly calm surface and that she had something to do with it. Thoughts of the night he'd kissed her heated and haunted her. Restless, she headed out to the horse barn and offered to help Meg with her classes. Looking outside of herself instead of always looking in provided her with a much-needed break.

Alisa drew a special joy from assisting with the

handicapped students. She could tell that every minute they spent on horseback provided them with a desperately needed feeling of progress. With her own memory returning at a slower rate, she easily identified with the need for progress because there were plenty of moments when she felt as if she was going nowhere.

More and more she craved independence and mobility. Five days into her last week at Dylan's, after work, she dropped by her apartment and decided to see if her car would start after two months of sitting. Sure enough, the dependable Honda revved to life with only two tries. Although the doctor had not yet released Alisa for driving, she decided to release herself. After leaving a quick, vague message on Dylan's voice mail, she drove to Granger's for her tutoring appointment.

After the tutoring session, she walked to the cottage she had shared with her mother. Sitting on the porch, she felt a dozen memories wash over her. The scent of chocolate chip cookies and dinner filled her mind. Her mother was an excellent cook. She remembered her mother stroking Alisa's hair at bedtime as she tucked her in. She remembered the long hours her mother had been forced to work and how she had often told Alisa that Alisa deserved better, and that one day things would be different.

Alisa hadn't really minded their small, cozy home. She had felt safe there. Although she'd missed her father's presence, Alisa hadn't felt deprived except for wanting sisters and brothers. As a child she'd sought a brotherly connection with the boys at the home. By the time her mother remarried, bearing more children was out of the question.

A breeze wafted over her face, stirring the heat of the sunny August day. Out of the corner of her eye she saw a cat jump onto the porch and settle into the shade. The sight of the tabby brought back yet another memory. Despite her mother's better judgment she'd allowed Alisa to keep a stray. *As long as that cat stays outside!* Alisa smiled. She could still. hear her mother's voice in her mind. Most of the time Alisa had complied. She'd only sneaked the cat inside on bitter nights, and Alisa was certain her mother had known. She'd merely turned her head.

Every time Dylan came around, he'd complained about the cat, but he'd always rubbed the tabby and made her purr. He'd complained because, in his opinion, the cat should have been a dog. When he grew up, he was going to have a golden retriever that would be the best, smartest dog in the world. Even now she could feel the longing in his voice. He'd wanted a dog so badly he could taste it.

Alisa thought of Dylan's beautiful, dogless home. She wondered what had happened to his dream of having a golden retriever. She wondered if that was one more loss suffered on his road to becoming a man. She wondered if he was unwilling to open his heart to the dog he'd wanted as a child.

* * *

Dylan glanced down his long driveway for the tenth time in as many minutes and began to sweat.

He knew Alisa should be fine driving, but he also knew she hadn't been behind the wheel in months and she was driving in downtown St. Albans during rush hour.

He couldn't help remembering how he'd felt when he'd first received the call that she'd been in an accident. He'd felt as if his blood had drained completely from his body. His chest tightened and he sucked in a deep breath. If anything happened to her...

If they stuck to the deal they'd made, she would be leaving in three days. Dylan felt ambivalent at the prospect. As each day passed, he found it harder and harder not to take what she had offered, not to touch her, not to fill himself with her. She was the one woman, the one person, who had made him feel not alone.

Perhaps it was best that the temptation of her proximity would be removed. After all, she would remember everything one day, he reminded himself. A cold chill passed over him despite the heat from the late-afternoon sun. One day soon she would remember everything. As surely as the seasons changed, one day soon her expression of longing would turn to contempt.

Squinting his eyes, he caught sight of her Honda as it rounded the curve. He breathed a sigh of relief.

"At least she didn't hurt herself," he muttered to himself.

She pulled to a stop a slight distance away and got out of the car and waved. "Look, Ma," she said in a joking tone, "I got wheels."

Dylan nodded. "So I see. You decided to ignore doctor's orders."

She nodded cheerfully as she walked toward him. "I did. What can I say? I've been such a good girl. This halo's getting too tight for my head."

His lips twitched at the same time he felt a tug of arousal. If ever a woman was both angel and bad girl, it was Alisa. He glanced at his watch. "I hesitate to ask where you went."

She climbed the steps and stopped in front of him. "Granger's and a couple other places." She studied his face. "I didn't do anything you wouldn't have done a week ago."

"What do you mean?"

"How long would you have followed doctor's orders if it meant you couldn't drive?"

Hell, he would've driven home from the hospital. "Not long," he conceded. "But I'm not a girl."

She blinked at him, then shook her head in disbelief. "You're not really going to be sexist about this, are you?"

He sighed. "It's not sexist. I just don't want you taking any chances."

Her eyes softened. She reached for his hand and hesitated. Despite all his good intentions, Dylan hated the hesitation. He knew the reason for it. She hesitated because he hadn't made love to her when she had asked him to in every way.

He took her hand and her gaze widened slightly.

"Life is full of chances," she said. "If you don't take some chances, you might as well be dead." She bit her lip as if slightly worried. "I took a few today," she said under her breath.

"A few," he echoed, wondering what was going on in her pretty head.

She smiled a shade too brightly. "When I visited Granger today, I remembered some more things."

Uneasy, Dylan waited. "Such as?"

"My cat," she told him.

He nodded. "Tiger."

"Yes, you complained about her, but you always rubbed her."

"She was so ugly I felt sorry for her."

"I'm not going to ask if that's why you put up with me as a child," she said.

He chuckled. "Okay."

She glared at him. "I'm just going to believe I was so adorable you couldn't resist me," she said. "Or my mother's cookies," she added. "Or the opportunity to see *The Lone Ranger* reruns. But that's another issue. I decided I wanted to get you a thank-you gift for all you've done for—"

Dylan stiffened and he dropped her hand. "Not necessary. You don't owe me anything."

She wiggled her hand as if she didn't know what

to do with it for a moment, then firmly clasped her hands together. "Well, I've already gotten it. I, uh, I really hope you'll accept it graciously and grow to like it." She paused a half beat and waited expectantly. "Will you?"

"Will I what?"

"Will you accept it graciously?"

He shrugged, uncomfortable, but unwilling to diminish the eager hopefulness he saw in her eyes. "Sure," he said with a shrug. "What is it?"

"Good," she said, infusing the single word with ten pounds worth of relief. Her gaze flickered nervously away. "It's in the car. Close your eyes."

"Why?" he asked, wondering if he'd voiced his acceptance too soon.

"Because I want you to," she insisted. "It's an easy thing to do. Won't cost you a dime. Just close your eyes," she said, lifting his hand to cover his eyes. "Promise you won't peek."

Silence followed. "Promise," she demanded.

Dylan stifled a groan. "Promise."

He heard the click of her heels on the stone walkway and steps, then the driveway. Her car door creaked open. "Don't peek!" she yelled.

"I'm not," he muttered, but he was tempted as hell. What had she gotten him?

She slammed the car door and quickly climbed the steps to stand in front of him. "Keep your eyes closed, but open your arms."

Confused, he frowned. "What—"

"Keep your eyes closed, but open your arms," she repeated.

"Okay," he said, his patience stretched. He immediately felt something furry and wiggly in his arms. Dylan looked down into the face of a fuzzy golden retriever puppy. His childhood flashed back to him and he remembered a time when he'd wanted a dog so badly he could taste it. That had been close to twenty years ago. The puppy looked at him with soulful caramel eyes and promptly peed on his Italian loafers.

Swearing under his breath, he looked at Alisa as if she'd lost her mind.

She winced at the puppy's "mistake." "Oops. I guess we'll have to work on that." She gave a smile and lifted her shoulders. "Meet Tonto, the dog of your dreams."

Dylan opened his mouth to tell her this wasn't a good idea. He no longer considered himself a pet person. He'd grown beyond that. He didn't want that kind of attachment. He didn't want any attachment. The dog wiggled in his arms. Dylan looked into Alisa's eyes and couldn't find it in him to snuff out the eager light of hope he saw there. *Damn.* A thousand refusals stuck on the edge of his tongue.

Something was seriously wrong with him. He could refuse to make love to this woman, but he couldn't refuse her gift that had just turned his Italian leather loafers into Dumpster bait. "Tonto, you say," he said, looking at the animal that would likely be the reason he would need to replace every stick of furniture in his house within a year.

"Tonto," she said nodding. "That was what you'd always said you would name your dog. Your dream dog," she said, her gaze sliding down to Dylan's shoes. "With a little work."

Dylan felt the back of his neck tighten with tension. "What possessed you to get a dog for me?"

She laughed mostly to herself and glanced away. "Not having my memory has taught me how precious memories are. Getting back some childhood memories reminds me what a precious time childhood was. Nothing was perfect, but everything was possible." She looked up at Dylan. "Your life has become almost too perfect, but it seems like you've lost your possibilities and dreams. I wanted to give you a dream that would remind you of a time when you still believed in possibilities. Besides," she said, "he'll keep you busy after I leave."

Dylan knew Alisa had no idea that he dreamed every night that he could rewrite history. No dog could solve that one.

The following evening Alisa scurried around anxiously awaiting the arrival of Dylan's half brothers and sister. Even though she'd only received one response, she still asked the housekeeper to set the table for five.

Dylan was busy trying to console Tonto, who had

howled plaintively most of the previous night. Homesick, she suspected, as the puppy let out another howl.

The doorbell rang, and Alisa's heart leaped into her throat. As she hurried to greet the guests, she crossed her fingers that all three Remingtons would be on Dylan's doorstep. She opened the door to one and only one. Her stomach twisted. "Grant," she said, working to produce a smile. "Please come in. I'm pleased you could join us."

He nodded, glancing around the foyer as he entered. He wore a curious but reserved expression on his well-sculpted, perfectly bored face. She wondered if Grant resented the fact that his father's money had provided Dylan with the means to purchase this home. He shouldn't, she thought, in light of the fact that Dylan had been denied a father throughout his childhood. She took a mind-clearing breath and pushed the thought aside. Tonight was for mending. Tonight was for possibilities.

Alisa believed in the possibilities even if Dylan didn't.

The puppy let out another whimper and Grant cocked his head to one side. "Is that a dog?"

"New puppy," she said, leading him toward the den. "I think he misses Mom."

"What kind?" he asked with the barest trace of interest.

"Golden retriever. You want to see him?"

He shrugged his shoulders. "Sure."

"This way," she said, and led him to the Florida

room where Dylan was petting the puppy and talking to him in a low voice. He shook his head. "I hate to hear you cry, bud, but you have to get used to this kennel until you learn not to take a leak on the floor."

Clearly pleased with the attention, Tonto wagged his tail.

"Nice-looking animal," Grant said.

Both Dylan and the puppy looked up. Dylan met Grant's gaze. "Thanks."

Grant moved closer to pet the dog. "Did you just get him?"

Dylan nodded. "A gift," he said, and the word sounded a bit forced to Alisa. "Watch your shoes. Tonto's not particular."

Grant glanced from Alisa to Tonto back to Dylan, and a wry smile cracked his practically perfect face. He bent down to pet the dog anyway. "I always wanted a golden retriever."

"Then you have something in common with Dylan," Alisa said. "He always wanted one, too."

Dylan shot Grant a curious glance. "Why didn't you ever have one?"

"My mother had a poodle. She thought retrievers were too big for the house."

Dylan shrugged. "At least you had a poodle."

"My mother had a poodle," Grant corrected. "And that dog didn't like kids. I'm not sure my parents liked kids, either," he said with a wry chuckle.

At a loss, Alisa glanced at Dylan for help. He was

clearly lost in thought. "Your sister and brother were also invited, but we didn't hear from either of them."

"My brother's in Bangladesh finding himself, so I doubt he'll be showing. My sister is probably still having nightmares from having met Dylan at the cocktail party. She operates on the principle that if she closes her eyes long enough, whatever is bothering her will disappear."

"So why did you come?"

Grant cracked a smile. It was a shark's smile that gave her the willies. "I want something from you."

Dylan paused, then nodded with approval at his half brother's directness. "Good, because I want something from you."

This was all just a little too strange and cool for Alisa's taste. "Why don't we have some dinner before you two begin your negotiations? The cook has prepared an excellent meal."

"What about the dog?" Grant asked.

Dylan shoved the dog into the kennel. "Tonto will provide the dinner music," he said, and the puppy immediately began to whine.

From Alisa's point of view, the meal might as well have been a contest of wits. Dylan and Grant parried and feinted throughout each course. When the cook delivered the cherries jubilee, Alisa was delighted to see the end of it. She ate a few bites, then excused herself to her room, leaving Dylan and Grant to face off again.

Dylan requested after-dinner brandy from the cook,

then asked Grant if he preferred to take it on the outside verandah or in the den.

"Outside," Grant said. "I've been inside all day."

Dylan gave his half brother a measuring glance as he joined the man with a brandy. "So, what do you want?"

Grant raised his eyebrows. "You don't beat around the bush. I could like that about you," he said. "I want your votes and any enthusiasm you can muster to put me in the position of CEO for Remington Pharmaceuticals."

"Power," Dylan said, not at all surprised. "Why should I vote for you?"

"Because I know the company and I care more about it than anyone else." His eyes narrowed. "I may even care more about it than my father did."

"I don't know much about our father," Dylan said, unable to keep a hint of bitterness from his voice.

"He had his failings," Grant said. "But in the end he tried to do the right thing. It wasn't right that he hid his paternity of you until he died. I think he tried to make it right in his will."

"It's a funny thing," Dylan said, taking a sip of brandy. "When you're a little kid, you're not interested in money and mansions. All you want is a father."

"If it helps any, he wasn't a particularly good father. He wasn't interested. He didn't show up for athletic events or graduations. But he covered your college educa—"

"Oh, no, he didn't," Dylan corrected. "I got a baseball scholarship and took out the rest in loans that I paid off before your dad died."

Grant met his gaze and Dylan saw a flicker of respect. "Hmm. Baseball scholarship. You must have been pretty damn good."

"I played a lot of ball at the Granger's Home for Boys," Dylan said. "There wasn't a lot of money for anything else."

Grant sighed. "That's life. You got a bum deal with my dad. You got a good deal with the lady."

Dylan frowned. "Lady?"

"Alisa," he said. "I can't tell if the relationship is friends or more."

"It's complicated," Dylan said, and silently added, *none of your business.*

"She's one of a kind. If you get tired of her—"

"Save your breath," Dylan said. "That won't happen."

Grant shrugged. "I've told you what I want. What do you want? A bigger piece of the Remington fortune? More money? Intro into the country club?"

Dylan smiled. His half brother had clearly underestimated him. "No, I want your support to start a bioengineering research division of Remington Pharmaceuticals."

Grant did a double take. "That's pretty damn expensive."

"Yep. I've got start-up funding for the first year."

"From who?"

"A private charitable organization," Dylan said.

"That's a lot of money," Grant said doubtfully. "I don't know many people who want to part with that much for charity's sake."

Dylan grinned again and lifted his glass. "Then maybe you've been hanging around the wrong crowd. Do we have a deal or not?"

"You'll support me as CEO if I support the bioengineering research project," Grant clarified. "You'll need more than my votes."

Dylan nodded. "I have more than your votes."

Dylan watched a glint of surprise cross Grant's face. "How?"

"Favors," he said. "I've collected a few."

Grant studied. "You're smarter than I thought. I underestimated you."

"Don't worry about it. You're not the first. In fact, you might say it's one of those things that has served me well my entire life," Dylan said.

"So how do I know you're not going to try to stage a takeover against me?"

"Because I don't want to take over anything," Dylan said. "I just want one little piece of Remington to grow on my own. You were born and bred to the job, and that's okay with me. But by some little crazy twist of fate, I ended up with a seat on the board, and it's not enough for me to just sit."

Grant gave him a long, measuring glance, then seemed to make up his mind. He extended his hand.

"Deal," he said. "Next time we'll have dinner at my house."

Dylan felt a rush of triumph and surprise as he shook his half brother's hand. He could almost believe Grant meant every word, but Dylan wouldn't hold his breath. The most important thing was, he had what he wanted in sight.

Seven

From the staircase Alisa tentatively watched Dylan as he stared at the front door Grant had just closed behind him. This could be good or bad, she thought, and gave in to her curiosity. "How did it go?"

He turned around and grinned widely. "Great!" Rushing toward her, he grabbed her in his arms and swung her around. "Thanks to you."

Delighted but confused Alisa clung to him for dear life. "What do you mean thanks to me? It was your idea to invite Grant and the others to dinner."

He stopped, allowing her to slowly slide down the front of his body to stand on her feet. His chest was hard, his scent made her dizzy, and the look in his eyes dissolved her knees.

"But you gave me the idea by saying it might be to my benefit to spend some time with them in a different setting." He lowered his head and kissed her. "Thanks."

Alisa's heart hammered in her chest. His arms held her loosely against him, but she was all too aware of his closeness. All too aware of his vitality and masculinity. "You're welcome," she managed. "Does this mean you've had some kind of meeting of the minds?"

Dylan nodded slowly as if he still didn't quite believe it himself. "Yeah. He even said something about inviting me to dinner sometime, but I won't hold my breath. What's important is he has agreed to support my proposal for a research project for Remington Pharmaceutical."

Dinner. Alisa's heart and mind hung on the word. Maybe Grant was a little closer to accepting Dylan. "I'm so pleased," she said. "I wish the others had come, but—"

Dylan waved aside her concern. "I don't need the others. All I needed was Grant's support to give me a little extra weight. Turns out he wants my support so he can be CEO. I don't need the others."

Her heart tightened at his words. She couldn't help wondering if Dylan truly needed anyone. It seemed as if he'd built a world for himself where he was nearly self-sufficient. Could he ever need a woman for more than physical release? Could he ever need a woman so much he thought he'd die without her? A forbidden longing swept through her. What would it take, she wondered, to show Dylan that he didn't have to be self-sufficient?

"We did it," he said, his joy pulsing through him. Holding her with his gaze, he lowered his mouth to hers again, this time taking his time and her breath. He rubbed his lips from side to side, and like a gentle, sensual invasion he slid his tongue just inside her mouth.

Alisa felt a slow burn travel throughout her blood. She opened her mouth to him, willing him closer and deeper. Stretching her arms around his shoulders, she pressed against him, reveling in the sensation of his hard body. Distantly she felt him guiding her back against the wall. He slid his thigh between her legs, and she drew his tongue into her mouth. Gliding his hands down to her hips, he rolled his pelvis against hers, making her wet with the erotic promise of his movements.

A restless urgency caught in her chest and spread outward. She wanted more, so much more.

Dylan reluctantly pulled his mouth from hers and drew in a shallow breath. He swore softly. "All I did was kiss you and I'm so hard I could burst."

Alisa swallowed. "Makes you wonder what might happen if we were doing more than kissing," she murmured.

Dylan's eyes lit with dangerous desire. "You're making it damn hard for me to do the right thing."

"Maybe you're not doing the right thing," she

said, her heart pounding. ''If I can drive a car, then I've recovered enough to—''

He covered her mouth with his hand, and something rebellious drove her to slide her tongue over his palm. He sucked in a quick breath and shook his head. ''I gotta get out,'' he said, pulling back. ''You—'' He swore again. ''I gotta get out for a little bit. I'll see you later.''

Alisa gripped the wall as she watched him leave. She was neither offended nor humiliated. The man had been so aroused he'd stuttered. While she didn't want to attempt walking at the moment, it was gratifying to know she wasn't the only hot-and-bothered one.

Her heart hammering in her chest, she felt a smile well up from her toes. She was getting to him. Inhaling deeply, she wondered if she had the guts to take the next step. She closed her eyes at the hot possibility. What if he rejected her again? What if he didn't?

The possibility tempted and seduced.

Alisa smiled again. She was getting to him.

Dylan took a mind-clearing drive to Justin's house to share his good news. Soon after he arrived, it became obvious that with the kids tucked in bed, Justin and Amy had a romantic evening planned. A sore reminder of what Dylan had left behind.

Dylan gave Justin a quick update, then took the long way home with the top down on his convertible.

He kept hoping the wind would blow some sense into his brain. His mind kept gravitating back to Alisa and how she'd felt in his arms. She'd kissed him as though she wanted all of him. Everything about her seduced him. The look in her eyes, the texture of her skin, even the way she breathed.

He struggled with the never-ending urge to slide inside her and take her again and again. She had been more girl than woman when he'd known her all those years before. Now she was the woman who haunted him and taunted him day and night.

He was still hard with wanting her. He swore. Just three more days until she was gone, he told himself. He would have done his duty and helped her recuperate without taking advantage of her. All he had to do was last three more endless nights, then she would be out of reach. Soon enough she would remember and hate him again for what happened years ago; he didn't want her hating him for anything he did now.

Thirty minutes later with his mind set, he pulled into his garage and walked into his house. Silence greeted him. He breathed a sigh of relief that Alisa hadn't decided to confront him or wait up for him. He checked on Tonto and found the puppy sleeping. *Thank goodness.* Dylan just hoped the dog's bladder would hold until morning. If ever he needed a full night's sleep, it was tonight.

He slowly climbed the steps and turned down the hall, stopping outside Alisa's room. He touched the wooden door and thought about the woman inside.

His gut began to ache. Pushing his needs aside, he dropped his hand and walked to his room. He would feel its emptiness more than ever tonight.

He pushed open the door and didn't bother with the light. Stripping off his clothes, he tossed them on the valet and turned back to his bed. But it wasn't empty.

In the near pitch-black darkness, Alisa knew the second he saw her. The air turned electric. Her heart raced.

"What are you doing here?"

"Waiting for you," she whispered.

He exhaled, but she could still feel his tension. It pulsed between them. "Why?" he demanded.

Alisa refused to shrink under his unwelcoming tone. "Because I want you and you want me."

He swore under his breath. "Why do you have to make this so hard?"

Taking her courage in her hand, she slid from beneath the sheet and scooted to the edge of the bed. She rubbed her mouth against his and her bare breasts against his chest. "Why do I make it hard?" she asked, trying to keep her tone light and teasing even though she found it difficult to breathe. "Isn't it my job to make it hard?"

"I don't want you to regret this," he muttered, sliding his fingers through her hair.

"A funny thing happens when you almost die, Dylan,'' she said. ''You don't want to miss anything. I don't want to miss you.''

His indecision shimmered between them for less than a minute, and Alisa waited to breathe.

''Oh, Alisa,'' he murmured, pulling her into his arms. ''So help me, I've been waiting for you for such a long time.''

In the corner of her mind she wondered how long he'd waited. Alisa had the sense that stones from his wall were falling down all around her. She clung to him as he took her mouth with pure passion. She felt the sizzle of it kick through her blood.

His was no easy, playful kiss. His mouth consumed her, demanded her response, and the wild force of his need made her head spin. He slid his hand down to boldly stroke her stiff nipple, then lower still to her bare rear end, undulating her intimately against his hardness. Everything he did told her he planned to take her in every possible way a man could take a woman. She shuddered in expectation.

''Touch me,'' he told her, seducing her with sensual, openmouthed kisses that made the air around them feel heavy with sexual expectancy.

Her breasts grew swollen beneath his touch. Lower, between her legs, she felt slick with arousal. Sliding her hands down the warm, smooth skin of his shoulders and chest, she made a vow to herself to memorize every nuance of him and this night. Somewhere inside her she knew this night would always be important to her. With that instinct, she pushed aside her inhibitions and resolved to make this a memory he too would never forget.

Lowering her head, she skimmed her tongue across his chest, then swirled around his nipple. He stiffened in response and she pressed her cheek against his chest to listen to the fast, heavy thud of his heartbeat. She allowed her hand to meander down over his abdomen and belly button, lower to the soft hair surrounding his hardness.

Although her need and his seemed to race through her like an oncoming freight train, she was determined not to rush. She felt him holding his breath, waiting for her touch. She fought the urgency and skimmed her hand to the side, caressing his hard thigh.

Lifting her mouth to his, she caught his muttered oath with her lips and made love to his mouth while she drew her hand closer and closer.

"When are you going to put me out of my misery?" he asked against her mouth.

"It's so good I want it to last," she said, and lazily guided her thumb from the base of his hardness all the way to the top. Swirling her tongue around his, she echoed the movement with her thumb on his erection, dragging his honeyed arousal around the swollen tip.

Dylan's groan vibrated inside her mouth. "Two can play," he warned and gently pushed her back on the bed. His knee pushed apart her legs and he drew her nipple into his mouth. "I love the way you taste," he said, and made her feel like the most desirable creature in the world.

He touched her waist and squeezed her hips, then lowered his fingers to her thighs and caressed her. He glanced the swollen bead of her sensitivity with one long stroke, then caressed her thigh again.

Alisa moved restlessly beneath him. He touched her again with one agonizingly slow and thorough stroke and again moved away. Alisa's pulse hammered throughout her body. The combination of his mouth on her breasts and his teasing fingers made her sweat. She bit her lip.

When he took the long intimate stroke again, the promise of pleasure was too great. She couldn't prevent her lower body from arching up to him. Her body was begging.

"You like that," he said in a voice rough with approval and began to stroke her. He slid a finger inside her and she felt herself go to the brink.

Frantic, she covered his hand with hers. "Not this time. I don't want to go that way," she said.

"Oh, Alisa," he said with a laughter that shimmied through every nerve ending. "You're going every way."

She touched his face, meeting his gaze. "Promise me," she whispered. "Promise."

Something deep, dark and timeless flickered in his eyes. "Promise," he said and kissed her.

He toyed with her, seeming to know exactly how to touch her, and she felt herself clench with pleasure.

As if from a distance, she heard him encouraging her in a low, velvet voice. Before she could breathe, he lowered his head down her belly and began to take her with his mouth. Alisa clutched the coverlet on his bed with her fingers as his wicked wonderful tongue drove her up and over again.

Weak with pleasure, she looked at him through a haze of wonder. She wondered why she had the sensation of familiar, yet new. Had she dreamed of this so often that she felt she knew him intimately?

He pulled a plastic packet from his nightstand and protected her, then entwined his fingers through hers. He lowered his head so that he was mere breaths from her face. "I promised I would go with you. Promise me you'll never regret this."

His low-voiced demand made her heart squeeze tight in her chest. How could she ever regret being with Dylan? She felt her eyes fill with tears. "That isn't possible. Not—"

"Promise," he said, and his eyes were full of a dozen emotions.

"I promise," she said, and he thrust inside her.

Alisa's breath stopped. His invasion was swift and sure. He filled her so completely that she felt over-stretched.

"I hurt you," he said, and began to pull away.

Alisa shook her head adamantly and slid her arms around his back to hold him tight. She took a careful breath. "It's just been a while," she finally managed. She licked her dry lips and willed herself to relax.

His dark gaze wrapped around her and held her. She heard him give a long sigh as if he were reining himself in. "So we'll go slow," he said, and moved inside her with an excruciating deliberate stroke.

Twining his fingers with hers again, he held her hands and every part of her inside and out. For those few precious moments she felt as if there was nothing between them. With each slow thrust he became more and more a part of her. Notch by notch he took her up the scale of arousal again. She could see by his clenched jaw that his restraint cost him.

The overwhelming sense of fulfillment echoed inside her heart, mind and soul. When he pushed her over the edge of pleasure again, she kept her eyes open and felt as if she were staring her destiny in the face.

He reached for her again in the middle of the night. A quick, hot coupling steeped in raw need that left her both breathless and sated. Then in the morning he made love to her slowly again, as if to savor her presence in his bed. He made love to her as if she were the most delightful surprise he'd ever found. His lovemaking made her want to be more to him, do more for him. Being this close to him made her want to heal all his wounds and make his wishes come true.

Afterward, with the sun shining through the curtains, she stared into his eyes and said, "I love you."

His eyes widened slightly and he took a quick breath. "You don't have to say that."

"But I do," she said, touching his face and wanting to touch his heart. "Why do you look so surprised?"

He shook his head. "I haven't heard that from anybody for a while."

"There's something I don't understand," she said. "This thing that's between us is so strong. I don't understand why we haven't been more involved with each other the last several years."

He glanced away and narrowed his eyes. She could feel the distance between them grow immediately. "It's complicated," he said.

"How?" she asked. "Tell me how."

He covered her hand, but still didn't meet her gaze. "I think you'll remember what you need when you're ready, and I think it would be better to remember things about us on your own."

"But—"

A dog's bark interrupted her.

Dylan chuckled. "My dream dog's bladder is probably about to burst. I'll take Tonto out," he told her and dropped a kiss on her lips. "You can rest a little longer."

Watching Dylan tug on his jeans and leave the room, she struggled with a sense of incompleteness. There was clearly a reason she and Dylan hadn't been more involved just before her accident, and he knew what it was. Sitting up, she closed her eyes and searched her mind for answers, but all she saw was a black void. She felt as if she were pounding on a steel door. She needed to know. Whatever had come between them was still hovering like an unwelcome ghost.

Grimly she sensed that whatever was in the past would continue to come between them unless she remembered it and banished it. If Dylan wouldn't tell her, then she would seek her information anywhere she could get it.

Eight

According to their agreement, Alisa should have left on Monday, but neither Dylan nor Alisa mentioned it. She wanted to stay, and although he hadn't spoken the words, his actions told her he wanted her to stay, too.

Dylan made love to her every night, but he stopped short at verbal professions. It was strange. Even though they didn't discuss it, Alisa felt a strong, underlying sense of commitment that flowed between them. She hoped she wasn't fooling herself.

Driven to know more about her preaccident experiences with Dylan, she visited the hospital psychiatrist and expressed her frustration over the blanks in her memory. He told her any number of things could trigger her memories. Then again, some of her emotions could block some of her memories for a while. He reminded her that she was still recovering and to be patient.

Alisa didn't appreciate being told to be patient, which indicated to her that she'd never been much for settling for the status quo, so she made arrangements to meet with Kate and Amy the following day. They met at a tearoom in downtown St. Albans, and Kate brought along her baby, Michelle. They ordered tea and cakes.

"Omigoodness, she's such a little lady," Amy said of Michelle as the baby daintily picked at the dry cereal Kate put on her high-chair tray.

Kate laughed. "She's probably good for about thirty minutes, then I'll need to bow out. She can scream with the best of them." She turned to Alisa. "I'm so glad you called us. I've been wondering how you're doing."

"Good for the most part," Alisa said, appreciating the warmth she felt from both women. "I'm driving, even though it terrifies Dylan. I've remembered my French enough to work and I've remembered a lot about when I lived at Granger. I'm having a tough time, though, with events that happened before the accident and was hoping you could help me."

"What do you want to know?" Amy asked. "Justin only had good things to say about you. When Justin and I were first married and I was afraid I'd made a huge mistake, you told me some things about him that made me look at him differently. You were always good with the kids.''

''Same here,'' Kate said. ''Michael always said you were the little sister all the guys wanted but never had. Except for Dylan, of course,'' she added with a smile.

''What about Dylan?'' Alisa asked.

Kate and Amy exchanged a look. ''What about him?'' Kate asked. ''He cared for you even more than Michael and Justin. You remember some of the things from Granger, don't you?''

''Yes, but I feel like there's something more,'' she said. ''I know there's something more.''

''I haven't known Dylan very long, but there's never been a time when you were around that he wasn't trying to get your attention. You weren't interested in him that way,'' Kate said.

''Maybe because of how we were involved as teenagers,'' Alisa mused.

''You remember that?'' Amy asked with wide eyes as she drank the tea and made a face. ''I don't like this stuff. I'd rather have a soft drink.''

''Then ask the waitress for one, silly,'' Kate said with a laugh.

''I will,'' Amy said, then turned back to Alisa. ''What do you remember about your romance with Dylan?''

''Not everything,'' Alisa said. ''When I still lived at Granger's, I remember sneaking out to meet him at night and we would talk and..." She shrugged, uneasy with revealing their private moments.

"And sneak a few kisses," Kate added.

Alisa nodded.

"And when you left?" Amy asked.

"I don't remember," Alisa said, thinking about the psychiatrist's words again. "I was told that my emotions might block some of my memories, particularly if it's something that upset me."

Amy nodded. "And do you remember anything from college?"

"I went to a girl's college. It was near a big public university. I wanted to major in art, but my mother and stepfather pushed French over art, so I got a minor in art instead."

"Do you remember dating in college?" Amy asked.

"Not much. I met my fiancé when I was finishing my last year."

"But you don't remember anything about Dylan while you were in college?"

"No. Why should I?" Alisa asked.

Amy seemed to hold her breath. Kate glanced at the baby. They knew something, she could see. They knew something she didn't know. "What do you know?"

"I don't really know anything," Amy said. "I haven't known Dylan very long, so anything I tell you would be third- or fourthhand."

"But third- or fourthhand is more than I have right now."

Amy exchanged another glance with Kate. She hesitated, and seemed to struggle with herself. "Justin got the impression you and Dylan got involved during college."

Alisa's heart tightened, but she continued to draw a mental blank. "How?"

"I don't know. I don't know the details. I was just led to believe that it didn't end well."

Alisa's stomach churned. She set down her tea cake and tried not to give in to an ugly feeling of foreboding. She tried to remain rational even though her feelings were strong. "Didn't end well," she repeated. "Well, that covers a lot of ground, doesn't it?"

Amy watched her carefully. "Yes, it does. Did I jog your memory?"

Alisa shook her head.

"Have you asked Dylan about any of this?" Kate asked as she shared a bite of cake with Michelle.

"Yes, but he says he thinks I should remember it on my own." She looked at each of the women. "It's time for some answers."

Kate's eyes grew solemn. "If you need anything, please call me."

"Same here," Amy said.

"I appreciate your truthfulness," Alisa told them. "I'm at a disadvantage."

"It's a tough situation," Kate said. "If I were you, I would want to know everything I could. At the same time, Amy and I only have hearsay. Dylan is the one who can tell you more. Plus, whatever happened between you happened years ago, and you're different people now. That should count for something.''

Alisa saw Kate's concern in her eyes, but with each passing moment she suspected that whatever had happened between her and Dylan was going to have a major impact on their future. Alisa felt like her past and future were speeding toward a head-on collision. She wondered if her heart would survive it.

After a long but successful board meeting, Dylan drove home and found Alisa on the veranda. The sight filled his heart. Sometimes he still had to pinch himself that she was with him. Jazzed by his recent success, he sneaked behind her, grabbed her and twirled her around.

She gave a little yelp of surprise, but her smile was full. ''What are you doing?''

''I have great news and you're partly responsible,'' he told her sliding her slim body down the front of his. The closeness reminded him of how it felt to hold her when he made love to her, which he planned to do again as soon as possible. ''I won approval for the research project.''

Her eyes widened. ''That fast?''

Dylan nodded. ''That fast,'' he said. ''Brother Grant was very vocal in his support, and I pulled in some favors.''

"Congratulations," she said, and lifted her mouth to his.

Dylan suspected she'd intended a brief kiss, but he wanted more. Having Alisa in his bed had been like providing oxygen to a part of him filled with burning embers. The more he had of her, the more hungry he became for her. He slid his tongue inside her lips to taste her sweetness, to feel her sigh. He felt the rush of arousal surging inside him and tamped down his impatience.

Pulling his mouth back, he rested his forehead against hers. "I want to celebrate with you."

"How?"

"I want to make love to you," he told her, and kissed her again.

He inhaled her scent and slid his fingers through her hair. She kissed him with passion, then pulled away and ducked her head beneath his. "We need to talk," she said in a husky voice.

"About?"

"I have some questions and I really need them answered," she said, and finally lifted her gaze to meet his. "You're the one with the answers."

Dylan felt his gut twist at the expression in her eyes. He would almost swear she remembered. If she had, however, he knew she wouldn't have kissed him just now. He also knew he could no longer wait for her memory to kick in. He would have to give her the truth she deserved.

Taking a deep breath, he pulled away from her and

went to the edge of the veranda. "What are your questions?"

"I've got some important gaps in my memory. One is when I was in college."

"You went to a small women's college," he said.

"I know that," she said, moving to stand beside him. She wished he didn't feel a million miles away. "I want to know what happened between you and me in college."

He looked at her sharply. "What do you remember?"

"I don't," she said, her anxiety doubling at the cold sound of his voice. "That's why I'm asking you!"

He narrowed his eyes and looked over the veranda "A bunch of your friends talked you into going to the nearby university to make the rounds at the fraternity parties. You told me you weren't wild about the idea, but you didn't feel like staying by yourself at the dorm. I don't know how many frats you visited before you visited mine, but I remember the moment I saw you walk through the door." He shook his head. "I couldn't believe it was you."

Alisa closed her eyes and tried to remember. She saw a hazy vision of herself walking through the doorway of a house packed with coeds dancing and partying. "I felt out of place."

"You looked like you did," Dylan said with a faint smile. "One of my fraternity brothers hit on you right away, but I intervened. You looked just as surprised to see me.''

''You got me a soda and we tried to talk, but the music was too loud,'' she recalled.

''So we sat out on the front porch,'' he said. ''I took you home and kissed you good-night. It was different than when you and I were teenagers.''

Alisa's heart bumped. She remembered the heat and promise in the kiss. She remembered falling in love with him again. As if the floodgates broke open, she was barraged with memories. She had been totally and completely in love with Dylan. ''We saw each other every weekend,'' she said. ''I wanted to be with you every minute,'' she said remembering how desperately in love with him she'd been.

With his fingers he gently lifted her chin upward so that she met his gaze. ''I wanted you every minute,'' Dylan said with an honesty that stole a piece of her heart. ''I wanted you so much it scared me. I started to need you, and I had learned early on that needing people was bad news, so I fought it.''

A sensual memory stole across her mind, heating her skin. ''We were lovers. No wonder I felt like—''

''Like what?'' Dylan asked, his eyes penetrating.

''When we made love a few nights ago, I felt like you knew my body. You knew how to touch me,'' she said.

His gaze darkened possessively. ''I've been waiting to make love to you for a long time,'' he told her.

Her heart hammered at the look in his eyes. "Why did you have to wait?"

He was silent for a long moment, and Alisa felt her mind whirl again. "I was crazy for you. What could have driven us apart?" she asked, looking away, trying to concentrate. "I remember my grades were sliding. I was having trouble with statistics." She covered her arms as she remembered snow covering the ground as she struggled with the concept of mathematical probability. "I had to get help and it still didn't make sense."

She felt Dylan's presence, but she remembered how worried she'd been about her grades. "I told you I couldn't see you," she said. "We fought. It lasted a couple of weekends. There was some kind of fraternity bash you wanted me to attend, but I just didn't feel like I could go. I hated having you angry with me, so I decided to surprise you," she murmured, recalling how she'd borrowed a friend's dress and begged for a ride to the university.

In slow motion Alisa saw her younger self all dressed up, eager to please, excited to surprise Dylan. "My hair was tied back," she murmured, wondering why her heart felt so heavy.

"With a black ribbon," Dylan added. "You wore a black satin dress."

"I walked through the fraternity house door. It was so loud. The music, the voices. Somebody was dancing on a table." She closed her eyes. "It smelled like everyone had taken a bath in beer." She remembered looking for Dylan, but not finding him. She'd asked several people and they nodded toward the back of the large room. She kept walking and finally saw him with his hands on a very pretty girl's hips. They'd been kissing, uninhibited carnal kisses. His body had been pressed against hers. Her hands had slid through his hair with intimate familiarity.

Alisa had felt sick. She felt sick even now. "You were kissing her," she whispered, opening her eyes and looking at Dylan in disbelief.

"She was kissing me," he said.

"I thought you loved me," she told him, the betrayal welling up inside her as if the event had just taken place.

"I did," he said, his face rigid.

"No," she said, the grief inside her overwhelming. "Me, singular. We had something so special. Why did you do that? How could you?"

He raked his hand through his hair. "It was eight years ago, Alisa. You knocked me on my butt. When you wouldn't come see me, I wondered if you were losing interest. I didn't plan it. I even thought about skipping the party, but my roommate talked me into staying. I drank a few beers and this girl kept after me."

Renewed humiliation crowded her throat. She had never felt so betrayed in her life. The visual of Dylan's mouth on the girl's slapped her again and again like a slide of the same picture again and again. She began to tremble.

"Alisa," Dylan said, reaching for her.

She pushed his hand aside. "No. I—" She swallowed over the old betrayal and new confusion. "I don't know what I expected, but it wasn't this." She shook her head. "Why didn't you tell me?"

"When?" he asked. "In the hospital when you were in ICU and your brain was swollen and they didn't know if you would live?"

She squeezed her forehead. "I guess not, but there must have been a time after I got out of the hospital."

"Your doctor encouraged me to let you remember things on your own. You didn't need any extra pressure. That's why I brought you here."

"But this was important. I should have known this. You should have told me before—"

"—before I found you in my bed and made love to you. Regrets, Alisa?" he asked with a dare in his voice.

She remembered the promise she'd made. No regrets. But she was confused and she felt deceived. "I need to think about this," she said, her chest tight and achy. "I need to figure out what this means. I need to—"

"—leave," he finished for her, and his face could have been made of stone. "You need to leave."

So she did.

Nine

———

Dylan didn't sleep that night. Or the next. He avoided his bedroom. Alisa's ghost was in the room. Her scent was still there. When he opened the door, he heard her laughter and felt her presence.

He'd been so careful, refusing to depend on her, constantly reminding himself that she would leave. He'd made a big mistake. He'd thought he'd protected himself, but somehow, some way, the worm of hope had burrowed inside him. Dylan had learned a long time ago that hope could be a killer. His mother had hoped his father would reappear and take care of them. He himself had hoped the same thing until he'd learned his lesson.

Hope was one of the strangest human emotions. It

was damn frail, but nearly hard to kill once it was growing inside a person. It led people to hang on in impossible situations, some situations best dismissed.

Although he'd fought it, there must have been some small, foolish part of him that had hoped Alisa would see him differently and keep seeing him differently. She had made him feel like the sun had come out again. She had reminded him of a time when he'd felt safe with her. He'd never felt that way with another human being.

Now she was gone again.

His heart felt heavy in his chest. His house felt hollow. Tonto whined and he cursed under his breath. The dog seemed to sense his unease. With a sigh he walked into the Florida room, grabbed a leash and took Tonto outside. He felt drops of rain on his face and ignored his discomfort.

He had survived without Alisa's love for eight years. He could do it again. He could go through the rest of his life without having her look at him as if he were the most important person in the world. His heart wouldn't stop beating. He wouldn't stop breathing. The world wouldn't stop turning.

His life would be the same as before her accident, he told himself, and hated the knowledge. He wished he hadn't made love to her. He wished he hadn't laughed with her. God help him, he wished he'd never known what it was like to have the love of Alisa Jennings because he sure as hell would never have it again.

* * *

"For somebody who just won over the Remington board of directors, you look like you might as well be going to a funeral," Justin said as the three members of the Millionaires' Club toasted Dylan's success at O'Malley's bar. "You should be happy as a clam. The Millionaires' Club is so committed to your bioengineering project that we won't have the funds to fund anything else for a long time."

"Maybe not," Dylan said. "The beauty of my project is that it will eventually earn money."

"I know how research works," Justin said cheerfully. "I'll be old and gray."

Dylan disagreed. "Do you remember a geeky little guy named Horace Jenkins?"

Michael squinted his eyes. "The name's familiar."

"Horace, Horace," Justin repeated, tapping his finger on the bar.

"He was a couple years younger than me. He didn't stay at Granger very long. Too smart," he said with a wry grin.

"What do you mean, too smart?" Michael asked.

"He was a genius. He scooted through high school in two years and got a scholarship to college, then got a triple doctorate in biology, physics and engineering. He's been teaching and working on a few inventions in his garage in his spare time."

"You dog," Justin said with a grin. "How did you find him?"

"I got him out of a bad situation one time. A couple of guys cornered him. I took a few punches for him and he never forgot it. He always kept in touch with me. Letters, then e-mails. He's not the most socially adept guy in the world, but he's brilliant. He's going to do some awesome things. He'll make Remington Pharmaceuticals a lot of money.''

''You got him on salary?'' Michael asked.

''With a bonus based on speed. But he's a scientist. He's not motivated by money.''

''What does he want?''

''Freedom to research without having to publish or teach.''

''How long has he been working on his inventions?''

Dylan smiled. ''Years.''

''Now that's what I wanted to see,'' Justin said. ''The trademark, Barrow lady-killer smile.''

Dylan felt his good humor fade. He shrugged and lifted his beer to take a long drink. He felt Michael's curious gaze.

''How's Alisa?'' he asked casually.

''Better. She's just about back to normal.''

Michael and Justin exchanged a glance. ''How normal?'' Justin asked.

The roar of conversation and tinkling of glasses struck an odd counterpoint to the quiet, hollowness inside him. ''She knows what happened. She's moved back to her apartment.''

Dylan felt the weight of their gazes.

''Sorry,'' Michael mumbled.

"Yeah," Justin said in agreement.

Dylan shrugged. "I knew it would happen. It was just a matter of time."

"How long since she left?" Justin asked.

"A few days." It had felt like a year.

"What did she say when you called her?" Michael asked.

Dylan stopped midmovement as he lifted his mug. "I haven't called her. She said she needed to think."

Michael looked at him like he was crazy. "And you're going to let her think by herself?"

"Well, yeah. If she'd wanted me around, she would have stayed."

Michael and Justin glanced at each other again.

Irritated, Dylan swallowed the last of his beer. "What?"

Justin cleared his throat. "I know you've dated a lot of women, but you haven't exactly been known for the duration of your male/female relationships."

"And you have?" Dylan challenged.

"I'm married to the woman I love," Justin said bluntly. "You're not."

Angry at the truth in his words, Dylan clenched his fingers into a fist and stuck his hand in his pocket. "So you're an expert on women."

Justin lifted his hand. "Not me, but I've learned a few things. One is you don't leave a woman alone if she's upset about you. It's called hedging your bet."

"He's right," Michael said. "Women have active imaginations. If I had backed off from Kate when we first got married, she would have left me so fast my head would still be spinning. Kate says it's one of those Mars/Venus things. Men need to go to their caves. Women need to talk.''

Dylan thought about their advice for a long moment, then shook his head. ''You didn't see the look on her face.''

Justin shrugged. ''If you don't mind living without her, then it's no big deal.''

''That's her decision,'' Dylan said crossly.

''Partly,'' Michael said. ''Depends if you're a quitter or not.''

Insulted, Dylan stiffened, almost rising to the bait. ''What do you mean quitter?''

''I mean no matter what happened in the past between you and Alisa, she won't forget that you were there for her when she needed you, unless you let her forget it.''

''I don't want her gratitude,'' Dylan said.

Justin rolled his eyes. ''Where is this sudden attack of honor coming from? You can use gratitude to your advantage. Do you want the woman or not? Are you gonna roll over and let her get away again? You already did that. Did it make you happy?''

''No,'' Dylan said.

''If you want Alisa, then you're gonna have to use everything to your advantage. You're not a twenty-year-old college kid anymore, and you need to make damn sure that she's reminded of that on a regular basis. It's my experience that one thing a woman wants is a man who's going to hold on to her no matter what. If you want this woman, you're in for the fight of your life. Trust me, I've just been through my own battle.''

Michael nodded. ''Same here,'' he said. ''It may sound hokey as hell, but I had to court my wife. Had to take her out on a date *after* we got married. After I did it, I found out it wasn't such a bad idea. But this is all up to you, bro. You have to decide if you're going to hold or fold.''

Alisa tried to examine her relationship with Dylan and pack it away in a nice, neat box, but every time she tried to categorize him as the man who had betrayed her, she couldn't help remembering that he was also the man who brought her markers and art paper while she was in the hospital. He was heartless, she told herself, then remembered that he allowed his property to be used for horseback riding lessons for handicapped children.

He couldn't be trusted, she told herself. Then why would her mind fly to his name if she ever had an emergency? She scowled as she cleaned out her bedroom closet on Wednesday night.

He didn't appreciate the importance of love. Perhaps, her conscience conceded, but what kind of permanent love had he ever experienced?

He didn't need anyone. Her stomach twisted at the thought. Closer to the truth. Dylan didn't seem to need anyone. She wasn't certain he was capable.

Straining to empty the corner of the top shelf, she came upon a small box and curiously pulled it down.

She wouldn't be able to keep his attention. The insidious thought slithered through her mind like a hissing serpent. Her chest tightened, and she tasted the familiar, bitter flavor of fear. The truth again. She told herself it didn't matter because she didn't *want* to keep his attention.

Pushing the unwelcome thought and emotion aside, she sat down on the carpet and pulled the top off the shoe box. It was full of letters, photos and stubs to movies, concerts and dances. The edges of some of the letters were charred as if they'd been rescued from a fire.

Alisa felt a sinking sensation. This was the Dylan box. She'd noticed that in her other photo albums there'd been no pictures of him. She'd found that curious until now.

She recalled the moment she'd begun to burn the memory of Dylan Barrow from her life. In the middle of the night at her mother's house, she'd crept downstairs to the den where the fireplace still burned. It had been weeks since her breakup with Dylan, but she still cried herself to sleep. She still was so angry she'd wanted to scream. To exorcise him from her mind and heart, she would burn the memories. She remembered tossing the precious mementos into the fire and watching them begin to burn.

Something inside her panicked. She wasn't quite ready to let go. Using the fireplace shovel, she salvaged most of the photos and letters and mentally put Dylan in a box. He had been her childhood friend and her first lover, so it was natural that he have a place in her memories. Alisa looked at the box and the small empty space on the top shelf. A small place in her memories, she saw, and put the lid back on the box.

The doorbell rang, and she shoved the box back in place, still unwilling to destroy that part of her history. She would have to think another time about why she still kept that box.

Hurrying to the door, she looked through the peephole and blinked several times. Dylan stood outside with a purposeful expression on his face. Her heart jumped. It was as if Dylan had jumped out of her box. She slowly opened the door.

"Hi," he said, when she didn't move from the doorway. "Can I come in?"

"Sure," she said, moving out of the way. "What's the occasion?"

"You've had time to think," he said, and walked into her den and sat down on her easy chair as if he belonged there. "Now it's time to talk."

Alisa felt an odd mix of emotions. She had thought about him entirely too much over the past few days. She had mentally screamed at him, cursed him and cried at him. Now that she had her opportunity, she was at a loss. "I'm not sure it's a good idea to talk."

"Why?" he asked, meeting her gaze so directly she almost looked away.

"Because of what happened between us," she said.

"Which thing?" he asked. "My teaching you to catch ball, you sneaking me into see reruns of *The Lone Ranger,* us tramping through mud puddles, me staying with you at the hospital, us making love when we were college kids or us making love as adults. Which thing?"

Alisa swallowed over a lump in her throat. Awash in confusion, she looked away. "I think what happened between us in college."

"That was one thing," he said.

"Big thing," she said, refusing to allow him to diminish it. "Big important thing."

"Agreed," he said. "You've had time to think about it. It's time for us to talk again."

Uncomfortable with his attitude, she frowned. "We didn't talk after it happened eight years ago."

"That was a mistake," Dylan said. "I made more than one mistake when I was twenty years old. I'm not going to make the same ones now."

Uneasy, she began to pace. "I don't really understand what you want. What happened between us in college changed things."

"Your accident changed things, too," he said with a level gaze.

She found his calmness maddening. "Temporarily," she said.

"Was it?"

Her chest grew tight. "Yes," she insisted. "As

soon as I remembered what happened in college, everything changed.''

''Everything?'' Dylan stood and walked toward her. ''So you have reverted to preaccident Alisa. You feel nothing for me.''

His voice purred over her skin, bringing her nerve endings to life. He stood so close, she thought, struggling with a thousand feelings she didn't want. ''I can't say that. Haven't you heard the expression 'been there, done that, got the T-shirt'? We've been there done that three times.''

''Then maybe we need to get it right this time,'' he said.

Alisa felt her heart pause, then take off for the races. ''I'm not sure this is a good idea.''

''Why?''

Heavens, he was making this difficult. ''I'll never be comfortable about you and your legions of feminine admirers.''

He lifted his lips in a sexy grin and dipped his head entirely too close to hers. ''Take me off the market,'' he taunted.

She took a quick shallow breath at his audacity. At another time she would have been sorely tempted to take him up on his seductive offer, but now she knew better. ''I might be able to take you off the market, but I don't think I have what it takes to keep you off the market. Someday, somehow I'll be busy taking care of some other part of my life and you'll feel neglected. And just because you're you, a woman will appear to console you.''

His humor faded. "Is that what you would expect from what you've come to know of me since the accident?''

That stopped her. Her mind went blank.

"If it is, you haven't been paying attention," he said with a finality that alternately terrified and relieved her. She wondered if the next words out of his mouth would be goodbye.

"But that's okay," he finally said, his jaw clenching with impatience. "I'm leaving right now, but I'll be back. A long time ago the old janitor at Granger used to joke with me and call me a 'bad penny.' A bad penny just keeps showing up. Well, Alisa, I'm your bad penny," he said, and turned toward the door.

Feeling as if she'd just been through a game of crack the whip, she skipped after him. "Why are you doing this?'' she asked to his broad, straight back. "Why are you talking when you know I don't want to talk? Why are you trying to get something started between us when I told you I don't want it?''

"I don't like the alternative," he said, then opened the door and stepped outside. He turned around to face her with a determined devil glint in his eyes. "*Hasta la vista,* baby.''

Alisa closed the door, then rested her back against it and slid to the floor. Whatever she had expected from Dylan, this wasn't it. All those years ago, when she'd sent him on his way, he'd gone quietly. Since then, when he'd occasionally asked her out and she of course had refused, he'd left her alone. Now he wasn't going quietly. How was she supposed to put herself and her life together if he was going to generate his unique brand of turmoil inside her all the time?

Frustration boiled inside her and she covered her eyes. "Great," she muttered. "Now I've got the terminator after me."

Ten

He called her every other day. Just enough to keep her off balance.

Alisa had filled in most of the blanks in her memory now and was trying to take back her life. She continued to work on crossword puzzles and make lists to help with her short-term memory loss. Her problem was that her preaccident life didn't quite fit. She had changed.

She wasn't sure what all those changes entailed, so she focused on putting one step forward and living one day at a time. She finished lacing her running shoes for an early-morning run, tucked her apartment key in her pocket and bounded out the door and down to the lobby.

She slowed, then stopped, but her heart raced. Dylan was waiting for her, dressed in a tank top, shorts and running shoes.

"What are you doing?" she asked, remembering that she'd told him she planned to start running this morning.

"Meeting you to go running," he said.

"Why?" she asked, moving toward the apartment building door.

"I could say it's because I love to run any chance I get," he told her, positioning himself closest to the street and matching his stride to hers as she began to run.

"Something tells me that's not true," she said.

"I don't want you having any more close encounters with SUVs," he said.

His words grabbed at her. She stopped and looked at him, taking in the stubborn set of his chin. Tenderness and frustration warred inside her. "I'm not going to get hit by an SUV again," Alisa told him.

"Damn right you aren't."

She sighed. "You're not responsible for me anymore. The doctor has officially released me."

"The doctor hasn't made love to you," Dylan said, his eyes dark with emotion, then he lifted his lips in a half grin. "Humor me. I just want to guard your body while you run."

Heaven help her, he made her feel so confused. She lifted her hands. "Okay, but it'll be short. I'm out of practice."

"You set the pace."

He ran beside her in blessed silence as if he understood her need to be quiet. Although she was always aware of his presence, after a few moments it didn't feel like an intrusion. He allowed her to choose the route and took a cool-down walk with her around her building.

"How are you doing?" he asked.

"Okay," she said. "Still trying to find my feet. That's part of the reason I wanted to start running again."

"Clears your head. Makes you feel stronger."

She nodded. "I miss my art," she confessed. "When I look at my schedule before the accident, it was packed. I didn't have time to draw or paint. You brought me the paper in the hospital and it was like finding a lost part of me."

"It was always your secret passion," Dylan said. "You hid it from just about everyone." He studied her for a long moment. "I'd like you to do a drawing for me."

"Of what?"

"Tonto, the dream dog with the pea-size bladder," he said dryly.

Alisa smothered a chuckle. "How's the training going?"

"My housekeeper almost quit."

She winced.

"But he's getting there. He's demanding and wants a lot of attention."

"I suppose you could have sold him," she said.

He shook his head. "He was a gift. Besides," he said with a sexy grin. "He's my dream dog. So when will you draw him?"

Just a little pushy, she thought, but she didn't feel at all put off. "I could probably do it sometime this weekend," she said.

"Great. Anytime except Friday night."

Her curiosity grew exponentially. It was none of her business what he did on Friday nights, she told herself, but she couldn't keep the question from popping out of her mouth. "You have plans for Friday night?"

His eyes glinted as if he could read her mind. "A charity fund-raiser. The entire board was invited. Would you like to join me?"

Wishing she'd kept her mouth shut, she shook her head. "No thanks," she muttered heading for the apartment building door.

"When will you run again?" Dylan called after her.

"Friday morning," she said. "But you don't—"

"I'll see you then," he said, and took off before she could tell him not to bother.

As she climbed the stairs to her apartment, she knew she drew a strange comfort from being with Dylan. He'd known her so long and he'd been there for her during that frightening, frustrating period after the accident. At the same time, she didn't want to depend on him. She might be able to trust him with her life, but deep down she wasn't sure she could trust him with her heart.

He'd broken her heart, and she couldn't let him do that again.

It was pouring rain on Friday morning, so she skipped her run and didn't see Dylan. That night her mind turned frequently to him. She wondered who he had taken to the charity function. Dylan never had to be without female companionship. The thought scraped at a raw spot inside her, so she pushed it aside and pulled out a sketch pad and lost herself in drawing for a couple of hours.

On Saturday morning Amy invited her to join her at the park with the children. Her red hair glinting in the sunlight, she patted the seat beside her on the bench. "Nice of you to come," she said, and pointed to the swings and wooden gym in front of her. "Perfectly positioned for watching."

Alisa joined the friendly, intense woman. "Nice of you to ask me. Did you have something on your mind?"

"A few things," Amy said glumly. "I hope nothing I said to you the other day made things bad for you and Dylan. I have a problem keeping my mouth shut sometimes."

"I appreciate your truthfulness," Alisa said.

"Yeah, but sometimes the truth hurts."

The truth had hurt, Alisa thought, but she would

rather live with the truth than a lie. "You're not responsible for what goes on between me and Dylan."

"I don't know what happened between you two in college, but he's a good guy," she said earnestly.

Alisa felt conflicted. Lately it seemed she always felt conflicted. "I'll figure it out," she said, and hoped like the dickens she would do it soon.

"Nick, use both hands on that sliding board," Amy called, rising to her feet. The newspaper she'd brought with her dropped to the ground. Alisa picked it up and saw the society column. She narrowed her eyes at the photo of Dylan.

Amy glanced down. "Oh, did you see that this morning?" she asked, sitting down again. "Can't blame the photographer. The man really does great things for a tux."

"Why is he in the—" Alisa broke off when she saw the write-up on the charity function. She skimmed the article. "'Charismatic Dylan Barrow made an appearance. No lovely lady by his side, but plenty of eager volunteers,'" she read and turned up her nose. "No surprise there. He always drew the women like bees to honey."

Amy arched her eyebrows in inquiry. "Now that you mention it, I seem to recall he usually had a different female escort whenever the occasion called for it."

"Yep," Alisa said, briskly closing the newspaper. Irritated by his ease with women and the fact that she cared, she folded the newspaper again.

"I guess that means he never got serious with any of them," Amy mused.

"I guess," Alisa said mildly.

"I don't think he ever got engaged or anything, did he?"

"Not to my knowledge," Alisa said, desperately wanting to change the subject.

"But you were engaged, weren't you?" Amy asked pointedly. She glanced at the kids on the playground equipment. "Two hands, Nick. One, two," she said to the little boy, then turned toward Alisa. "You were engaged, weren't you?"

"Yes," Alisa said. "He was older, very stable, very conservative." Everything Dylan wasn't, she thought.

"Do you remember why you didn't marry him?"

"I didn't love him enough," she admitted. Although she'd tried not to compare her relationship with her fiancé to her relationship with Dylan, she'd ultimately been unable to deny there'd been something missing.

"Hmm," Amy said. "Wonder what Dylan thought of that."

"We never discussed it," Alisa said, and wished she wasn't discussing it now.

Amy shrugged and smiled. "Probably doesn't matter now. The other reason I invited you here was to ask a big favor."

Alisa saw that Amy had suddenly turned nervous. Curious, she watched her. "What's the big favor?"

"If you can't do it, I'll understand."

"Okay. What is it?"

She made a face. "I hate to ask people to do things for me. Justin's always fussing at me about it."

"Amy," Alisa said. "What is it?"

Amy exhaled. "Justin and I would like to go away for a long weekend, but we need someone to take care of—"

"I'd love to take care of the children. Just tell me when," Alisa said.

Amy's eyes filled with unshed tears, and she threw her arms around Alisa. "Thank you. It's a lot to ask, but they're basically good kids. We wanted them to feel as secure as possible before we took a trip together, but with this round of chicken pox, Justin and I really want to get away."

Alisa remembered that Amy had adopted the children after her sister and brother-in-law had been killed in an automobile accident. She admired the woman for her strength and determination. "I'm glad you asked me. When are you planning to go?"

"In two weeks," she said, and put her hands together as if saying a prayer. "As long as everyone stays well. A minihoneymoon in Belize," she said, and her eyes glowed with anticipation. "I'm so excited I don't know what to do. But I'm sure Justin will help me think of something."

Alisa felt a pinch of longing at the obvious love on Amy's face. "You really turned Justin around, didn't you?"

Amy turned thoughtful. "He turned me around, too. I used to think that being alone meant strength. Self-reliance was the most important thing to me. Justin taught me that it was okay to count on someone else. We both got lucky. It's a once-in-a-lifetime thing, that's for sure."

Alisa's mind turned to Dylan. Once in a lifetime, Amy had said. Her heart squeezed tight. She wished things could have been different. She wished— She broke off the dangerous, seductive thought. Wishing could get her into trouble.

"I'm warning you. He isn't going to pose," Dylan said as he tussled with Tonto on the Florida room tile. "Ouch!" he said, and pulled his hand away. "Puppies may be cute as hell, but their teeth are like razors."

Tonto immediately looked forlorn and tried to push his head up under Dylan's arm.

"Come here, gorgeous," she said, kneeling. The dog perked up his ears and rushed her. Her drawing supplies spilled all over the floor. Tonto grabbed a brush in his teeth.

"Oh, no, you don't," she said, and the puppy began a game of tug-of-war. "Don't you have a sock for him or something? This dog needs some toys."

"Toys?" Dylan poured a basket of dog toys on the floor. Distracted, Tonto abruptly dropped the brush.

"Thanks. Sheer volume often works with males," she said.

Dylan tossed her a sideways glance. "Are you speaking of toys or something else?"

Alisa shrugged. "Just about everything. Toys, cars, women."

He nodded toward Tonto as the puppy burrowed through the pile of playthings. "He has a favorite. Watch," he said. "He'll pass up all the others to get his favorite."

Sure enough the dog stopped searching when he found a squeaky rubber cat. Tonto plopped down on the floor and gnawed the toy.

Dylan met her gaze. "You were saying something about volume?"

Alisa dodged the question. "I think it might be best for me to take some photos and just watch him for a while. Can I borrow your camera?"

"Sure," he said with a thoughtful expression that let her know she hadn't fooled him with her change of subject. Alisa accepted the reprieve and spent the next half hour taking pictures of the puppy indoors and out.

"How does he know not to leave the backyard?" she asked when she observed that Tonto stayed within a specified area.

"Electric fence," Dylan said. "After I chased him all the way to the horse barn, I knew I had to do something. He's coming along," he said. "You made a good choice."

Alisa was quietly pleased that her impulsive gift to Dylan had enriched him. She glanced over the beautiful green acres of his estate and felt a twinge of homesickness. Impossible, she told herself. She didn't feel as if she belonged here. Especially with him.

"I should go," she said.

"Why?" he asked.

Irritated, she noticed that he asked that a lot lately. "Because I'm done taking pictures and observing Tonto."

"So now you can relax with me," he said, moving close to her.

Alisa's heart thumped. What a joke. She couldn't relax with Dylan. She opened her mouth to refuse, but he covered her lips with his fingers.

"Tell me a secret," he said in a low seductive voice that reminded her of the hot nights they'd shared in his bed. "Tell me how to persuade you to stay."

Fighting the steamy memories and a shot of panic at the way her mind was wandering, she stiffened her knees and her resolve. "I'm not going up to your bedroom with you," she said breathlessly.

Surprise lit his eyes. He grinned that terrible grin that disabled women by the droves. "I wasn't going to ask you," he said.

Feeling immediately foolish, she covered her hot cheeks with her hands "Oh, well—"

Dylan covered her hands with his. "I'm waiting for *you* to invite me to your bedroom."

Her contrary mind zapped her with a quick, hot visual of Dylan naked in her bed, filling her mind, filling her body. "Don't hold your breath," she said.

He tilted his head to one side and considered her. "You're remembering what it was like when we made love in my room, aren't you? You can do more than remember, Alisa."

Flee, flee, flee temptation! She backed away from him. "Save your flirty come-ons for your droves of admirers. They don't work with me. I'm not sweet little adoring Alisa anymore."

His gaze darkened. "I know by firsthand experience that you're not little Alisa anymore. Even without that experience, I've seen what's in your lingerie drawer. No angel wings there," he said. He lowered his face to within an inch of hers. "As for my droves of admirers, I haven't noticed them. I'm too busy with you."

Shaken, but determined not to show it, Alisa lifted her chin. "Well, you can consider yourself unbusy with me," she said, and turned on her heel. She felt his hand circle her wrist, and he spun her back around.

"All these sly comments you keep making about my imaginary harem could get pretty damn old."

"Women are like potato chips to you, Dylan. You can't eat just one."

He rolled his eyes. "You're so clever. Here's a news flash. Just like you're no little adoring angel, I'm no player, no—"

"Cheat?" she suggested in a cool voice.

"That's right," he said, clenching his jaw. "And the sooner you accept that fact, the better we'll get along."

"We don't need to get along," she told him.

He took a breath as if he was struggling for patience. "That's where you're dead wrong," he said. "But you'll learn. It may be the death of me, but you'll learn."

Alisa left his house angry enough to spit. She dropped off the film at a quick developer on the way home and decided to wait. After she collected the film, she grabbed a bottle of wine, some brie and bread, and a candy bar.

As she walked through the door of her apartment, she headed straight for the kitchen, got a glass for the wine and a knife and plate for the brie and bread. Making a face at Dylan even though he couldn't see her, she took her goodies to her bedroom. It was the one room where she felt most comfortable.

Plopping down on the bed, she poured a glass of white wine for herself and took a long cool swallow. "Delicious," she said, relishing the pleasure and telling herself that Dylan wasn't a necessary ingredient for her to enjoy her life. When she thought of sensual pleasures, however, her mind stubbornly visualized Dylan.

Wrinkling her nose, she shook off the mental picture and resolved to replace it with real pictures of Tonto. She opened the freshly developed photos and smiled at the friendly retriever. The dog was a handful, but a beautiful handful. *Like his owner?*

Alisa chuckled to herself. Dylan would love being compared to a dog. She flipped through the photos and caught sight of one with Dylan laughing. Something inside her pushed her toward him. She lingered over the sight of the light in his eyes, his white teeth, and his heart-melting features. She scanned the next two photos and found another of him, his gaze thoughtful, intense. She'd seen that expression on his face many times. He was a complex man. Not everyone knew that about him, but she did. He was fascinating. There had been a time when she couldn't know him enough. She still had more than her fair share of curiosity about him.

Why? she wondered, frustration picking at her. She knew more about Dylan than most anyone else. Why was there more she wanted to know?

She poured another glass of wine and nibbled on the brie and bread as she looked through the photos again. After a few moments she picked up her pad of paper and began to sketch. But it wasn't Tonto's image that appeared on her pad. It was Dylan. She started with one image she'd gleaned from the photos and sketched Dylan. She looked at it critically and frowned. It wasn't quite right. It didn't capture the essence of him. Remembering another facial expression that had intrigued her, she ripped the first sketch off the pad and let it fall to the floor. She began again. Hours later her pad was empty and her floor full of sketches of Dylan.

Dylan continued to join her when she ran in the mornings. Alisa tried to snub him, but the effort made her feel small. Another way the accident had changed her, she supposed. Dylan may be the question mark in her life that never got answered, but he didn't deserve poor treatment.

The time drew near for her to take care of the children for Kate and Justin. Alisa was looking forward to a weekend filled with children's books, finger painting, Disney movies, popcorn and cookies. She packed a bag and heard children's voices and the sound of a piano playing as she rang the doorbell at Amy and Justin's home.

The three-and-a-half-year-old twins answered the door and stared at her. "We can't let you in," Nick said.

Jeremy nodded. "We'll get in trouble."

"Can you get Amy?" Alisa asked.

"She's real busy," Nick said, and Jeremy nodded.

Alisa sighed. The first thing she would need to cover with Amy was the temporary transfer of power or she was going to spend a lot of time standing on the front porch this weekend.

"What about Justin?" she asked.

"He's not to be 'sturbed cuz he's playing stocks and making lots of money," Nick said.

"Emily?" she asked doubtfully.

The boys lit up and yelled at the top of their lungs. "Emily, Alisa wants you!"

Emily appeared at the door and smiled.

"Any chance I can come in?" Alisa asked.

Emily nodded and immediately opened the door.

Nick gasped. "You're gonna get in trouble. You're not supposed to let people in the house."

"I won't get in trouble. Alisa's taking care of us while Aunt Amy and Justin go on a honeymoon."

"I wanna go on a honeymoon," Jeremy said glumly.

"You're still gonna get in trouble," Nick said.

"Will not," Emily said.

"Will, too," Nick said.

"Will not to infinity," Emily said, silencing him with her advanced retort.

"What's infinity?" Nick asked suspiciously.

"It's bigger than the biggest number you can think of."

"I wanna go on a honeymoon," Jeremy said.

Alisa could see the beginning of separation sadness in the small boy and felt a tug on her heartstrings. She put her arm around him. "I brought cookies for everyone who isn't going on a honeymoon."

Jeremy's eyes widened. "Cookies? Lots of cookies?"

She gave him a quick squeeze. "Lots, but not enough to make you sick. We can finger paint and read and play games and watch movies."

"And go horseback riding," a deep voice from behind her said.

Alisa whipped her head around to see Dylan just inside the front door. How had he gotten in so easily after she'd stood on the porch for four minutes? She stood. "What are you doing here?"

"I'm helping take care of the kids while Justin and Amy use my condo in Belize," he said calmly.

"That's not possible," she said. "Amy asked me to take care of the kids this weekend."

"And Justin asked me," Dylan said.

Alarmed, frustrated, Alisa shook her head. "But—"

"Hey, these kids are great, but they're a handful. I'm guessing Justin and Amy decided two heads would be better than one."

He shrugged. "Looks like we're both baby-sitting. I'll let you have the master bedroom," he told her, and leaned closer to speak in a voice just for her ears, "but don't even think about sneaking into my bed in the middle of the night."

Alisa opened her mouth to protest, but he continued whispering.

"Just because we'll be together for three nights doesn't mean you should remember what it was like for me to touch you and you to touch me. It's a waste of time for you to remember how good it was when we made love to each other."

He pulled back. "Don't even think about trying to seduce me or distract me. I need my sleep," he told her and strode past her as she watched him with her mouth hanging open.

Eleven

Alisa's visions of a cozy weekend with the children got flushed straight down the toilet. Glancing at Dylan's broad back, she scowled. She didn't want to spend an entire weekend with the man she was trying to stuff in a box.

Amy appeared in the den with a suitcase and cast a nervous glance at Alisa and Dylan. "Sorry about the mix-up on the arrangements," she said. "Justin asked Dylan and I asked you, and after we thought about it, we thought this crew might do better with two adults. Do you mind too much?" she asked Alisa more than Dylan.

"We're fine," Dylan said before Alisa could speak.

Alisa surreptitiously shot him a disagreeable look,

then took a deep breath. Amy was clearly nervous about leaving the children. Alisa didn't want to add to her uneasiness. "I'm sure we'll be fine."

Justin sauntered into the room jingling his car keys and carrying his suitcase. All smiles, he shook Dylan's hand. "A weekend in Belize at your condo. I owe you for this," he said.

"My pleasure," Dylan said. "Drink a Beliken beer for me."

Nick and Jeremy raced in front of Justin and Amy. "We're gonna go horseback riding," Nick said.

Emily trailed behind her brothers.

Amy knelt down in front of the children. "You are going to have so much fun," she said. "Now make sure you do everything Alisa and Dylan tell you to do. And don't fight with each other." She gave each child a tight squeeze. "I'll be back before you know it."

"When will you be back?" Emily asked.

The uncertainty in the little girl's voice made a lump form in Alisa's throat. The children had lost both their parents in the same accident, and the loss they'd battled was tremendous.

"Monday," Amy said, stroking Emily's hair. "You can call me anytime. Dylan has the phone number. You help Alisa, okay?"

Emily nodded and clung to Amy. Jeremy returned for a second hug. "Can I go on the next honeymoon?" he asked.

Amy's eyes filled with tears. "Next time we'll take a family trip and everyone will go," she said.

Alisa saw the potential for a cryfest and was determined to head it off. "I need some cookie testers," she said. "I'm still not sure I've got this recipe just right."

Jeremy appeared front and center. "I'll be a tester."

"Me, too," Nick yelled, then gave a quick squeeze to Justin before he followed Alisa to the kitchen.

Dylan shooed Justin and Amy out the door, and the weekend officially began. After a lunch of sandwiches and cookies, Alisa cleaned up the kitchen while the children played in the backyard. Dylan tossed the trash in the can.

"I didn't know you liked children," she said to him.

He met her gaze. "Why wouldn't I? I was a kid once."

"Well, you don't have any children."

"And I damn well am not having any unless I'm married," he said heatedly, then shook his head and brushed his finger over her nose. "There are lots of things you don't know about me, Alisa. You haven't been paying attention for a long time."

She wanted to deny it, but she couldn't. With the exception of her recuperation after her accident, she had done her best not to pay attention to Dylan. She felt a surprising pang and wondered what she'd missed.

"Are you the same girl you were at eighteen?" he asked in a low voice.

She immediately shook her head. "No."

"I'm not the same guy I was eight years ago, either."

She couldn't argue his reasoning. Food for thought when she was already full. She would think about it later. "We should probably check on the kids," she said, and hurried outside to where the children played on an elaborate swing set that occupied half the backyard. After making sure everyone took a trip to the bathroom, she and Dylan situated the kids in the car and drove to his estate.

They walked to the barn and met Meg Winters and the already saddled horses. At first the children were overwhelmed by the size of the animals.

"He's awful big," Jeremy said of Sir Galahad, his wide-eyed gaze filled with wariness.

Nick nodded. "He's really tall. I want to ride the little one."

Jeremy nodded, still not quite sure. "You go first," he said to Nick.

Nick shook his head. "You can go first," he said with uncharacteristic generosity.

"Emily should go first. She's a girl," Jeremy said.

Emily shook her head and backed away. "I want to watch."

Meg Winters smiled. "The horses look big, but they're very nice. Come and meet Sir Galahad."

Meg introduced the kids to the horses, allowed

them to feed them apples and helped them feel more at ease. After a few minutes Nick was willing to try a short ride on the pony, but Jeremy was still reluctant.

Alisa wrapped her arm around the little boy's shoulder. "Don't you want to go for a ride, sweetie?"

"He's so big. What if I fall?"

She gave him a reassuring squeeze. "We won't let you fall. Would you like me to walk beside you?"

He nodded, and seemed to hold his breath as Dylan placed him in the saddle. Alisa led Sir Galahad for a slow walk in the field. After a short time she returned.

Emily's little face was filled with a mixture of longing and fear. Dylan was whispering in her ear. She nodded hesitantly, then Dylan mounted the mare and Meg lifted Emily up to sit with him in the saddle.

"Emily's riding with Dylan," Nick said with excitement. "I wanna ride with Dylan."

Alisa watched Dylan hold Emily securely in front of him, allowing her to hold the reins at the same time that he held them. He talked to her in a low, reassuring voice.

The image froze in her mind. On several occasions he had spoken to Alisa in that same reassuring voice when she'd been frightened. He had held her so many times. Her heart swelled in her chest. She wondered what Dylan's children would look like. Would they be adventurous like him? Would his son drive all the girls crazy with his smile?

What would Dylan's wife be like? she wondered,

and found the very thought of him marrying hurt. Would his wife see past his wealth to the man he was? Her heart tightened in her chest. Why should any of this matter to her? Confused, she reminded herself that she certainly wasn't the woman who could hold his attention, so she needn't be thinking about it.

After the horseback ride, Dylan and Alisa took the kids swimming. The children were so active they had to watch them every minute. The kids played with Tonto, and Dylan grilled hamburgers for dinner. When the sun set they returned home. After baths the children were so tired they nearly fell into bed.

Alisa felt ready to fall down, too. She sank onto the sofa in the den and closed her eyes while Dylan got a beer from the refrigerator. She heard him return and felt him lift her feet at the end of the sofa so he could sit down.

"This is just the first day," she said, surprised at how tired she was. "I can't believe their little bodies hold so much energy."

"And it was only a half day," Dylan said.

"I'm trying to figure out how Amy was a teacher and then came home to take care of kids, too," Alisa said in wonder. "But women in all kinds of careers do it every day. I'm surprised she and Justin didn't move to a larger house after they got married."

"They wanted the kids to feel secure, so they didn't make any changes," Dylan said. "I better hit the road."

Alisa opened her eyes and stared at him. "You're not leaving?"

He shrugged and took a swallow of beer. "You said you wanted to do this by yourself."

Alisa pictured herself taking care of the kids with no help for the next three days and felt her stomach dip. "I might have been a little hasty."

"Really?" He glanced at her with the ghost of a sexy grin. "Is that your sweet way of saying you need me?"

She took a breath and struggled with her pride. Sitting up, she drew her knees against her. "I'm conceding that in this case two adults are definitely better than one."

"Even if I'm the other adult," he concluded.

She threw him a dark look. "I suppose this is when I should tell you that you really surprised me with Emily today. You were wonderful with her."

"With all my experience with females, I'm surprised you're surprised."

"I didn't mean it that way," she said. "You were very sensitive and gentle with her." She paused as similar memories trickled through her mind. "It reminded me of how gentle you were with me when I was a little girl."

She didn't reach out to him, but she wanted to. He didn't touch her, but she could see that he wanted to.

"You made it easy," he said, and his words and the look in his eyes touched her. The moment swelled between them, brimming with shared memories and history and unspoken emotion. His gaze fell over her in what she'd almost swear was a longing way. She felt an echo of the same longing inside her.

"We were a good team today?" he said, knocking back the rest of his beer. He stood and strolled toward the door.

She nodded, strangely reluctant for him to go but unwilling to ask him to stay. "We were."

"I'm going to bed," he said, and met her gaze. "Remember not to think about me tonight. Remember not to remember," he told her.

His admonition was like striking a match over a vat of gasoline. She was immediately consumed with memories of what it had been like to be held by him, to make love with him. Damn him, he wouldn't stay in her neat little box.

It rained on Saturday, and Dylan watched as Alisa pulled out her bag of tricks. Books, games, finger painting and more books. When the kids grew edgy in the afternoon, she exchanged a look of desperation with Dylan.

"Television," he suggested in a mock-serious tone. "With all this emphasis on reading, kids just don't get enough television these days."

She chuckled and the sound warmed him. Dylan resisted the urge to touch her, but he was getting damn tired of resisting.

"I'm saving TV for when I have zero working

brain cells left. Everyone, put on your old tennis shoes,'' she said.

''What do you have planned?'' he asked.

She smiled at him mysteriously. ''Hey, when it comes to rainy days, I learned from the best.''

''Walking in the rain and stomping through mud puddles. Cleanup's gonna be he—'' He broke off when she shook her head at the swear word he almost used. The kids had big ears. ''Hellacious,'' he said.

''I'd rather have a tough cleanup than grumpy kids. But you can stay inside if you're afraid of getting wet,'' she said with a challenge in her eyes that made him want to haul her over his shoulder and carry her home. Someday, he promised himself. Someday.

Later that night, after dinner and a Disney flick, Nick and Emily drifted off to sleep without a problem. Jeremy, however, was still wide awake after the fourth book Alisa read to him.

''What do you usually do at bedtime?'' Alisa whispered to the little boy.

''Go to sleep,'' he said.

Dylan smothered a chuckle at the look of consternation on Alisa's face.

''What do you do when you have a hard time going to sleep?'' she asked.

''I listen to songs,'' he said. '''Kum-ba-yah' and 'Ninety-nine Bottles of Beer on the Wall.'''

She bit her lip. '''Ninety-nine Bottles of Beer on the Wall'?''

Jeremy nodded. ''Justin sings it to me.''

Alisa glanced at Dylan, and it took him a moment before he grasped the direction her female mind was headed. He shook his head. "Absolutely not," he said in the most forceful whisper possible.

"But he's used to a male voice," she said, brimming with amusement.

"Lower yours," he said.

"Just think of it as counting sheep for him," she said, then added, "musically."

Groaning, Dylan walked to the side of the boy's bed and sat down on the floor. He looked into Jeremy's wide open eyes. "I'm warning you I don't sing very well."

Jeremy patted Dylan on the head. "That's okay. Justin can't, either. That's why I fall asleep so fast."

With those words of encouragement and Alisa's barely muffled snicker, he began to sing, if one used the term loosely, "Ninety-nine Bottles of Beer on the Wall" and didn't stop until he was down to seventy-three bottles. He watched Jeremy's chest rise and fall with sweet, even breaths. Sleep, blessed sleep.

He glanced up to meet Alisa's gaze and caught a tenderness in her eyes that made his heart stop. In that moment she was closer to loving him than she had been in eight years.

She finally looked away and he breathed again. Dropping a kiss on Jeremy's forehead, she stood and nodded toward the door. They walked out of the room and after closing the door, drew a collective sigh of relief.

"I cannot tell a lie. I'm very impressed," she said.

"You didn't know I could sing," he said, leaning sideways against the wall beside her.

She bit her lip. "I still don't know you can sing."

"You're impressed that I know all the words to 'Ninety-nine Bottles of Beer on the Wall,'" he concluded tongue-in-cheek.

Alisa rolled her eyes. "No, I'm just impressed you did it. You didn't want to do it, but he needed you to sing tonight."

"It could have been a purely selfish move," he told her. "Jeremy's sleep equals Dylan's sleep."

She tossed him a skeptical glance and leaned closer to him. "Maybe, but I think it was pretty terrific of you to sing Jeremy to sleep."

"How terrific?" Dylan asked.

"Very terrific," she said. "Why?"

"Will you give me a good-night kiss if I finish 'Seventy-two Bottles of Beer on the Wall'?"

Alisa looked horrified. "I'll give you a good-night kiss if you promise not to sing 'Seventy-two Bottles of Beer on the Wall.'"

"Deal," he said, and lowered his head.

She turned her head and gave him a quick peck on the cheek. Dylan didn't say a word. He just met her gaze and stayed where he was. Her eyes glinted with an array of emotions: passion, longing, doubt. Oh, how he hated seeing the doubt.

Slowly she lifted her mouth to his and he knew this was the sweetest offering he could receive. She didn't completely trust him, and that knowledge burned in his gut like a hot iron. But she wasn't denying she wanted him.

Resisting the urge to claim and consume, he kissed her gently. He savored the soft texture of her mouth and just barely dipped his tongue across her silky inner lips. She swept her tongue over his, and again he forced himself to hold back. In the soft light of the hall he felt the door to her heart crack open. It was a fragile moment he was determined to handle with care.

He balled his fists to keep from touching her. His body clamored with the need to feel her against him, but he denied himself. Her soft sigh made him ache, but he rubbed his lips against hers once more, then pulled back.

He heard her intake of breath, and she licked her mouth as if she liked the taste of him. The erotic, involuntary gesture nearly sent him over the edge. "Good night Alisa," he said, instead of throwing her over his shoulder and taking her to bed.

"G'night, Dylan," she murmured, and walked away from him, leaving him with a longing that wouldn't quit.

The following day the sun shone brightly, so Alisa and Dylan repeated a visit to his estate with horseback riding, a swim in the pool and playing with Tonto. Although the high activity level suited the children, Alisa could tell they were missing Justin and Amy.

She began to talk about how they would need to get ready for their return on Monday by cleaning the house and perhaps baking some cookies. By nighttime the children had straightened their rooms and were primed to start baking in the morning.

Alisa read an extra story to Emily while Dylan sang again. Afterward she followed the sound of soft music downstairs and found Dylan in the den with two glasses of wine. His feet propped on an ottoman, he waved her into the room. "A toast," he said, apparently anticipating her question. Rising, he brought her a glass of wine. "The kids survived and so did we."

She laughed in agreement, and he clinked his glass to hers. Alisa took a sip of the cool, clear liquid. It was so good she drank it quickly and was surprised to feel a little buzz.

"More?" he asked.

She shook her head. "It was very nice, but I think one glass is enough."

"I'll only have two," he said. "I may have to give an encore presentation. I sang down to eighty-three bottles of beer on the wall." He set down his wine and stood in front of her. "Dance with me," he said.

Off guard, Alisa didn't know what to say. Her instinct was to say no. And yes.

"Just one dance," he said. "I've always liked this song."

He took her in his arms and Alisa tried to listen to the song over the beating of her heart. A woman's pure voice floated over a guitar and mandolin singing about a love that was spoken more from action than words.

She fought the spell moving over her. She tried to cling to logic and good sense, but Dylan's arms felt solid and secure around her. His scent was familiar in a wholly sensual way. She closed her eyes, and for a few moments the music and the man transported her away from pain, away from herself.

His longing for her hung in the air around them, reassuring her, seducing her.

"Come with me to Belize next weekend," he murmured in her ear.

Surprise raced through her. She opened her eyes. "What?"

"Go with me to Belize. It's a long weekend, and I want to be with just you."

Her heart hammered in her throat. Another adventure with Dylan. She wanted to go. She wanted to be with just him, but a slice of doubt and pain cut through her. What if she trusted him and shouldn't? What if she believed in herself and shouldn't? Her chest felt tight and heavy, and she was filled with contradictory thoughts.

"I can't," she finally said, pulling back from him and hating that she was hurting him. "I could trust you with a million things. I wish I could trust you with me."

Twelve

Dylan's invitation dangled seductively in the back of Alisa's mind. Even after Justin and Amy returned from their trip clearly refreshed and she and Dylan parted, Alisa couldn't stop thinking about his invitation to go to Belize. When they were children, the invitation could have been to go stomping through mud puddles, but the idea was the same. Another adventure with Dylan. For Alisa he had been the ultimate adventure.

She wrestled with good sense and doubts all week. She deliberately made herself remember how terrible she'd felt all those years ago when she'd seen him with that college coed. For some reason, though, she was unable to hang on to the hurt and sense of betrayal quite as easily as she once did.

Friday arrived and she was still conflicted. She watched the clock pass the time he'd told her he would be leaving. Although he'd made it clear he wanted her to come with him, he'd also made it clear he was going with or without her.

She was nowhere near the airport, but she could see him boarding the plane and fastening his seat belt. The flight attendant would pay him extra attention, she thought with a trace of darkness. She could hear the roar of the engines and feel him soar into the air. Without her.

The phone rang and her heart raced. Maybe it was him? Alisa snatched it from the cradle. "Hello?"

"Alisa, darling, Mother, here. When are you coming home so I can see that you are totally okay?"

Alisa swallowed a sigh. She'd been in touch with her mother over the past two weeks since her mother's return from Europe. Her mother had been appalled to learn of her accident and had wanted to visit Alisa to make sure her daughter was fine, but Alisa had wanted a little more time. "Soon, Mom. Maybe next weekend."

"What's wrong with this weekend? It's Labor Day, after all, and I bet you have an extra day off on Monday."

"I do, but I thought I'd avoid the travel headaches. How is Louis?" she asked, referring to her stepfather.

"He's fine when he takes his blood pressure medication." Her mother paused. "Darling, I don't want to pry, but you don't sound happy."

Alisa smiled sadly to herself. Her relationship with her mother had certainly had its ups and downs, but even so, she could hide very little from her mom. "Dylan invited me to go to Belize with him."

"Oh," her mother said and the one word oozed heavy disapproval.

"I said no."

"Well, I think that was wise. You've been through a difficult time and you're still a bit vulnerable. Dylan just can't be counted on."

Alisa chafed at the words. "He has actually been very good to me since the accident. He visited me in the hospital every day and insisted I recover at his home."

"I know, but in the long run, who knows what he'll do?"

Her mother's doubt echoed her own, but she felt compelled to defend him. "He's a good man. He has grown in a lot of ways."

"He hurt you terribly," her mother reminded her.

Alisa felt the familiar stab of pain, but she just couldn't wallow in it like before. "He did hurt me, but that was one time, a long time ago."

"But you deserve better," her mother said.

"That sounds snobby, Mom," Alisa said.

Her mother sighed audibly. "I wish you had gotten married when—"

"I didn't want him enough," Alisa said, and the rest of her sentence hung between them. She hadn't wanted her fiancé, but she did want Dylan. "I need to go. I'll talk to you later. Okay?"

"I need to see my daughter," her mother said.

"Soon," Alisa promised, and hung up the phone. She needed to talk to someone with some perspective. Someone who didn't dislike Dylan but knew he had flaws. She glanced at the clock and knew Kate and Amy would be busy with their families. Maybe she could try to see them tomorrow. She called Amy first, and the woman must have sensed Alisa's distress. She immediately offered to meet her that night at a bar close to her house.

Alisa was surprised to see Kate at the table with Amy as she walked through the door.

"Ladies' night out," Amy announced with a wide smile.

"I feel guilty taking you two away from your families on a Friday night," Alisa said.

"Don't," Kate said. "The guys put in a video for the kids in one room while they sneaked into another room to watch a Braves game. Amy had us over for dinner."

"I would have invited you, too, but I wasn't sure if you would end up in Belize," she said, raising her eyebrows. "So do we need to get you tipsy or are you ready to talk?"

"If ever I needed a clear head, it's now," Alisa said.

"Okay, I'll order a cosmopolitan for myself," Amy said and leaned back in her chair. "So tell us why you're in St. Albans instead of Belize. I can testify from personal experience that it's a wonderful place to go.''

Tense and uneasy, Alisa pushed her hair behind her ear. ''I don't know what to do about Dylan.''

''Do you love him?'' Kate asked.

''Yes.''

She blinked, then smiled. ''Have you checked the airlines?''

''He has never said he loved me,'' she confessed.

Amy looked surprised. ''Hmm. You mean aloud?''

''What do you mean?''

''I mean Dylan may have never said he loved you aloud, but if you look at his actions, he has screamed it.''

Alisa took a moment to digest that.

Kate leaned toward Alisa. ''These guys are so confident and successful it's easy for us to forget that as children they never had anyone they could count on. Commitment is scary for them because they've never seen it work out in their own lives.''

Alisa felt a surge of her own fear. ''I'm afraid to believe in him,'' she confessed.

Kate looked at her with sympathy. ''But you love him. So, what's the alternative?''

''Protecting myself, distancing myself, trying to get past him,'' she said, although she didn't know if she'd ever truly succeed. She wasn't sure she wanted to live without Dylan. The mere idea felt as if she would be cutting out a huge part of herself.

"Is there any chance you could find what you have with him or something better with someone else?" Kate asked.

Alisa thought for a long moment, but the answer came right away. "No. I need to check the airlines, don't I?"

Amy nodded. "The feelings I had for Justin scared me so much all I wanted to do was run in the other direction. When I finally ran to him, I wasn't scared anymore."

Her heart in her throat, Alisa left on a flight the next morning at the unearthly time of 5:30 a.m. and schlepped through three connections. The last was a puddle jumper from Belize City to the island of Amber Gris Caye.

The island was filled with couples, and the horrible thought hit her that he might not be alone. Banishing the notion from her head, she reminded herself this trip was a risk she was willing to take. Her nerves coiled into a tight knot. Armed with the address of Dylan's condo, she rode a golf cart from the tiny airport through the dirt streets until she arrived at a well-kept property of white two-story buildings with red roofs. Bougainvillea bloomed at every turn. The island breeze beckoned her toward the ocean, and she decided to look for Dylan there.

Dylan knocked back the last of his third Beliken beer, put the bottle beside him and leaned back in his lounge chair. Belize offered the best breeze in the world. He was convinced it was therapeutic, and if he was lucky it would temporarily blow thoughts of Alisa from his mind. Every time he thought of her, he ached. He deliberately closed his eyes.

"Just tell me you're here by yourself," a woman's voice said.

Alisa's voice. He was imagining things. He shook his head. Hell, he'd needed this trip more than he'd originally thought.

"I said just tell me you're here by yourself. They told me the puddle jumpers back to Belize City don't fly after dark."

Dylan opened his eyes and saw her standing at the end of his lounge chair. She was holding a piece of luggage in one hand, and she might not know it, but she was holding his heart in the other. He blinked. "If you're a mirage, baby, keep talking," he said, and rose from the chair.

"No mirage. I'm real," she said, and added, "real scared."

He shook his head. "Don't be. Don't ever be scared with me." He pulled her into his arms, unable to believe she'd come. "When did you change your mind?"

"After I argued with my mother and told her what a good man you've become."

Dylan's heart squeezed so tight he almost couldn't breathe. He damn well couldn't speak.

"After I realized you're the curse that is my cure.

I still haven't sketched Tonto yet because I used all my paper on you. I thought I was exorcising you from my soul.''

He pulled back to find tears in her eyes. "But you didn't.''

"No.'' She shook her head, her voice breaking. "My soul was trying to tell me how much I love you. You are the one man who has been everything to me, my brother, my friend, my protector, my lover.''

"Omigod,'' he said, because it couldn't be true. She was the wish he couldn't make, but she'd somehow come true. His own eyes filled with tears. "Omigod,'' was all he could say.

He kissed her and their tears mingled on their cheeks. He tasted the salt and wanted to taste her the rest of his life. Suddenly, holding her against him wasn't enough. He swept her up in his arms and strode to his condo just a few feet away. Pushing the door open, he kissed her again, then kicked the door shut behind him.

There was too much inside him to say, too much not to show. She kissed him as if she meant forever, and Dylan felt a volcano of passion roar through him. They didn't make it to the bedroom. He pulled off her clothes and she hastily helped rid him of his swimsuit. Her urgency drove him on.

"I love you, Alisa,'' he said, following her down on the sofa. "I want to be your everything forever.''

Watching her precious face, drinking in her no-doubts gaze, he thrust inside her and sealed his declaration.

Two months later Dylan and Alisa were married in the chapel at Granger Hall where it all started. Justin, Amy and their crew were there along with Michael, Kate and Michelle. Happiness was bubbling over. Even Alisa's mother had accepted Dylan as a son-in-law. After they said their vows, the guests adjourned to a lavish hotel reception.

They ate, they danced, and when Alisa tossed her bouquet, it fell into Horace Jenkins's hands. The befuddled, brilliant researcher hadn't known what to do.

Dylan sneaked her away from the party into a closet for a few moments alone. Alisa glanced at the linens piled on the shelves and started to laugh. "Was there something you wanted to talk to me about?"

"Yeah. This day is a miracle for me," he said. "Nobody's ever loved me enough to make a promise to stay with me forever."

Alisa's throat knotted with emotion. There was so much she still wanted to give him. So much she would give him. "I guess that makes me the luckiest person in the world, doesn't it?"

His eyes grew shiny with unshed tears, and he shook his finger at her. "You weren't supposed to do that," he told her.

"Do what?"

"This was supposed to be my turn to tell you how much I love you and how important you are to me."

"Oh," she said, touching his cheek. "When do I get my turn?"

"Tonight in your bed in that little black silky thing I saw in your lingerie drawer."

She smiled. Even though they'd made love in her bed several times, Dylan had insisted they spend their wedding night there. "Does that mean you want me to stop telling you how much I love you?"

"Never," he said, taking her in his arms. "Never stop. And I never will, either."

* * * * *

*Be sure to watch for
Leanne Banks's short story*

THE MONARCH AND THE MOM

*to be included with short stories by
Sharon Sala and Marie Ferrarella
in the very special upcoming anthology*

LABOR OF LOVE

On sale in July 2001 from Silhouette.

THE FORTUNES OF TEXAS

invite you to meet

THE LOST HEIRS

**Silhouette Desire's scintillating
new miniseries, featuring the beloved**

FORTUNES OF TEXAS

and six of your favorite authors.

A Most Desirable M.D.—**June 2001**
by Anne Marie Winston (SD #1371)

The Pregnant Heiress—**July 2001**
by Eileen Wilks (SD #1378)

Baby of Fortune—**August 2001**
by Shirley Rogers (SD #1384)

Fortune's Secret Daughter—**September 2001**
by Barbara McCauley (SD #1390)

Her Boss's Baby—**October 2001**
by Cathleen Galitz (SD #1396)

Did You Say Twins?!—**December 2001**
by Maureen Child (SD #1408)

And be sure to watch for *Gifts of Fortune*,
Silhouette's exciting new single title,
on sale November 2001

*Don't miss these unforgettable romances…
available at your favorite retail outlet.*

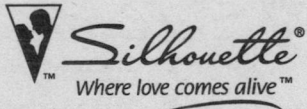

Where love comes alive™

Feel like a star with Silhouette.

We will fly you and a guest to New York City for an exciting weekend stay at a glamorous 5-star hotel. Experience a refreshing day at one of New York's trendiest spas and have your photo taken by a professional. Plus, receive $1,000 U.S. spending money!

Flowers...long walks...dinner for two... how does Silhouette Books make romance come alive for you?

Send us a script, with 500 words or less, along with visuals (only drawings, magazine cutouts or photographs or combination thereof). Show us how Silhouette Makes Your Love Come Alive. Be creative and have fun. No purchase necessary. All entries must be clearly marked with your name, address and telephone number. All entries will become property of Silhouette and are not returnable. **Contest closes September 28, 2001.**

Please send your entry to: **Silhouette Makes You a Star!**

In U.S.A.	In Canada
P.O. Box 9069	P.O. Box 637
Buffalo, NY, 14269-9069	Fort Erie, ON, L2A 5X3

Look for contest details on the next page, by visiting www.eHarlequin.com or request a copy by sending a self-addressed envelope to the applicable address above. Contest open to Canadian and U.S. residents who are 18 or over. Void where prohibited.

Where love comes alive™

Our lucky winner's photo will appear in a Silhouette ad. Join the fun!

HARLEQUIN "SILHOUETTE MAKES YOU A STAR!" CONTEST 1308
OFFICIAL RULES
NO PURCHASE NECESSARY TO ENTER

1. To enter, follow directions published in the offer to which you are responding. Contest begins June 1, 2001, and ends on September 28, 2001. Entries must be postmarked by September 28, 2001, and received by October 5, 2001. Enter by hand-printing (or typing) on an 8 ½" x 11" piece of paper your name, address (including zip code), contest number/name and attaching a script containing 500 words or less, along with drawings, photographs or magazine cutouts, or combinations thereof (i.e., collage) on no larger than 9" x 12" piece of paper, describing how the Silhouette books make romance come alive for you. Mail via first-class mail to: Harlequin "Silhouette Makes You a Star!" Contest 1308, (in the U.S.) P.O. Box 9069, Buffalo, NY 14269-9069, (in Canada) P.O. Box 637, Fort Erie, Ontario, Canada L2A 5X3. Limit one entry per person, household or organization.

2. Contests will be judged by a panel of members of the Harlequin editorial, marketing and public relations staff. Fifty percent of criteria will be judged against script and fifty percent will be judged against drawing, photographs and/or magazine cutouts. Judging criteria will be based on the following:

   - Sincerity—25%
   - Originality and Creativity—50%
   - Emotionally Compelling—25%

   In the event of a tie, duplicate prizes will be awarded. Decisions of the judges are final.

3. All entries become the property of Torstar Corp. and may be used for future promotional purposes. Entries will not be returned. No responsibility is assumed for lost, late, illegible, incomplete, inaccurate, nondelivered or misdirected mail.

4. Contest open only to residents of the U.S. (except Puerto Rico) and Canada who are 18 years of age or older, and is void wherever prohibited by law; all applicable laws and regulations apply. Any litigation within the Province of Quebec respecting the conduct or organization of a publicity contest may be submitted to the Régie des alcools, des courses et des jeux for a ruling. Any litigation respecting the awarding of a prize may be submitted to the Régie des alcools, des courses et des jeux only for the purpose of helping the parties reach a settlement. Employees and immediate family members of Torstar Corp. and D. L. Blair, Inc., their affiliates, subsidiaries and all other agencies, entities and persons connected with the use, marketing or conduct of this contest are not eligible to enter. Taxes on prizes are the sole responsibility of the winner. Acceptance of any prize offered constitutes permission to use winner's name, photograph or other likeness for the purposes of advertising, trade and promotion on behalf of Torstar Corp., its affiliates and subsidiaries without further compensation to the winner, unless prohibited by law.

5. Winner will be determined no later than November 30, 2001, and will be notified by mail. Winner will be required to sign and return an Affidavit of Eligibility/Release of Liability/Publicity Release form within 15 days after winner notification. Noncompliance within that time period may result in disqualification and an alternative winner may be selected. All travelers must execute a Release of Liability prior to ticketing and must possess required travel documents (e.g., passport, photo ID) where applicable. Trip must be booked by December 31, 2001, and completed within one year of notification. No substitution of prize permitted by winner. Torstar Corp. and D. L. Blair, Inc., their parents, affiliates and subsidiaries are not responsible for errors in printing of contest, entries and/or game pieces. In the event of printing or other errors that may result in unintended prize values or duplication of prizes, all affected game pieces or entries shall be null and void. **Purchase or acceptance of a product offer does not improve your chances of winning.**

6. Prizes: (1) Grand Prize—A 2-night/3-day trip for two (2) to New York City, including round-trip coach air transportation nearest winner's home and hotel accommodations (double occupancy) at The Plaza Hotel, a glamorous afternoon makeover at a trendy New York spa, $1,000 in U.S. spending money and an opportunity to have a professional photo taken and appear in a Silhouette advertisement (approximate retail value: $7,000). (10) Ten Runner-Up Prizes of gift packages (retail value $50 ea.). Prizes consist of only those items listed as part of the prize. Limit one prize per person. Prize is valued in U.S. currency.

7. For the name of the winner (available after December 31, 2001) send a self-addressed, stamped envelope to: Harlequin "Silhouette Makes You a Star!" Contest 1197 Winners, P.O. Box 4200 Blair, NE 68009-4200 or you may access the www.eHarlequin.com Web site through February 28, 2002.

Contest sponsored by Torstar Corp., P.O Box 9042, Buffalo, NY. 14269-9042.

Silhouette Books
invites you to mosey on down to
Jacobsville, Texas—home of the best-looking,
sweetest-talking men in the entire
Lone Star state!

DIANA PALMER

LONG, TALL *Texans*

Calhoun, Justin & Tyler
(On sale June 2001)

Featuring the men you can't get enough, this
collection is a treasure for all fans. Contained
in this fabulous volume are the first three
Long, Tall Texan tales ever told! Relive the
passion. Revel in the breathtaking romance.
And rejoice in the triumph of true love!

You won't want to miss this special
3-in-1 collection by international bestselling
author Diana Palmer!

Available only from
Silhouette Books
at your favorite retail outlet.

Silhouette®
Where love comes alive™

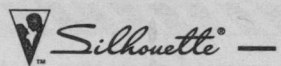

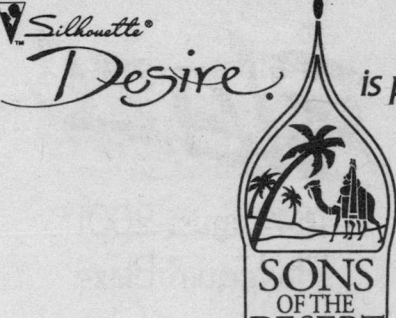

Silhouette Desire *is proud to present*

SONS OF THE DESERT

THE SULTANS

Powerful sheikhs born to rule and destined to find love as eternal as the sands.

In three breathtakingly sensual new romances, Alexandra Sellers continues her bestselling series, Sons of the Desert. Love and adventure are the destiny of the three grandsons of the late Sultan of Bagestan, who must fight to overthrow a ruthless dictator and restore the sultanate.

Look for these exciting stories:

The Sultan's Heir
(Desire #1379—July 2001)

Undercover Sultan
(Desire #1385—August 2001)

Sleeping with the Sultan
(Desire #1391—September 2001)

Available at your favorite retail outlet.

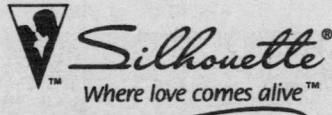

Where love comes alive™

NOTORIOUS
Vicki Lewis Thompson

In August 2001
Harlequin Blaze
ignites everywhere...

TWO SEXY!
Stephanie Bond

GOING FOR IT
Jo Leigh

Look for these red-hot reads
at bookstores!

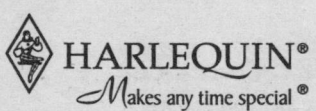

EXPOSED
Julie Elizabeth Leto

HARLEQUIN®
Makes any time special ®